THE NYrIan
Transmission

THE NYRIAN TRANSMISSION

Christopher McMaster

Southern Skies Publications

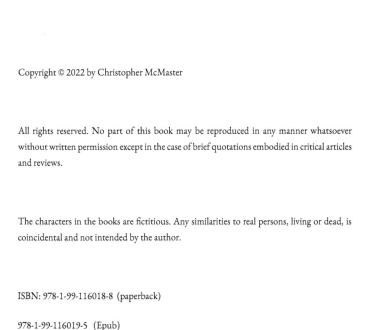

ISBN: 978-1-99-116018-8 (paperback)

978-1-99-116019-5 (Epub)

www.southernskiespublications.com

Cover art: Vila Design at: www.viladesign.net

First Printing, 2022

For WI

One day, you will find that pairing soul. It will be a feeling beyond your imagination. You just can't help it but to adore them. You will feel your whole heart melt for this person. This beautiful soul will bring joy, laughter, calmness and so much inspiration, that you will finally see hope in front of you. For once, you can actually say, I'm in love. I can see a future with this person. I can share my life with this person. Maybe this one is not a lesson. Maybe this one is what they call a soulmate.

Carlos Medina

Time travel used to be thought of as just science fiction, but Einstein's general theory of relativity allows for the possibility that we could warp space-time so much that you could go off in a rocket and return before you set out.

Stephen Hawking

Love is space and time measured by the heart.

Marcel Proust

1

Alan winced as the needle pricked his skin. He closed his eyes and tried to relax. He imagined he was a prisoner on death row, finally strapped to the gurney where the lethal injection was administered. He read somewhere that's how they used to do it. Animals killing animals. But that was most of human history, wasn't it? Smart monkeys, that's all they were. Very smart monkeys.

Games sometimes helped this part, helped prepare him for what came next.

He felt his body sink into the gel foam of his chair, and he took his mind to the sensation, the soft cradling of heel, calf, back of knee, thigh and buttocks. He memorized the muscle groups once, thinking that might help him cope. It didn't. As the weight increased, the words slipped from his grasp, and it was all he could do to hold onto consciousness.

The gel filled the space at his lower back, wrapped around the latissimus dorsi, cupped the deltoid and trapezius, and like a lover's hand held the splenius capitis. *Trust me*, it said, as if he had a choice.

His head sank back. He once imagined that foam as a woman's thighs, his head nestled in her inner softness. It was distracting, which was the intention, until she began to squeeze and he felt as if his skull was going to explode. That wasn't pleasant. Months after returning from that voyage a lover tried to ask what he was worried about. She tried valiantly not to take his reluctance to place his head in that area personally, and he tried to please her. Both failed.

He later, thankfully, got over it. But not with her.

Now he imagined death. Acceleration always felt like a kind of death. The needle entered his vein. He brought all his attention there, cold and hard, his flesh pierced and his body laid bare, vulnerable. If these were his last moments, which they might be, he wanted to experience it as fully as possible. To be in the moment. Every moment. Every sensation. He felt a rush of fluid force its way into his body and climb his arm. He followed it as it flowed into his chest, hit the heart and then coursed towards his brain and through his torso. The chemicals were warmer and heavier than blood, and his mind dispersed throughout his body with the potion.

If these were his last moments, would he feel fear or regret? With the potent chemical spreading to vital organs and poisoning his body, his time fleeting, his life ending, what would fill his mind? Alan focused more intently on every sensation, divining an answer. The needle retracted, leaving only a sore rawness where it had been. A warmth spread from his chest and pushed downward as the weight of acceleration increased. He tried to stay with the heat, take his mind to it, but as the pressure intensified, his attention seemed to flatten, to spread and run. He went to his breath, trying to watch it go in and out, his last breath—surely, he would hold onto that? But in the end, he simply tried to keep breathing.

And then the chemicals kicked in. His heart sped and his lungs expanded. He gulped air, or tried to. In reality, his lungs weren't expanding, they were merely becoming more efficient at extracting oxygen from the little he took in. His legs twitched as stimulants flooded his muscles. He lost sight as his eyes rolled back, only to clear seconds later, his vision unnaturally clear. He stared at the ceiling, wheezing, as the ship picked up speed and his body weight doubled, and then doubled again.

Knuckles began to prod and poke, hard nubs built into the chair, driving into his flesh. He took his mind to each sensation, but there were too many, moving too quickly from shoulders to feet, and feet to shoulders. They seemed random, but each point on his body probed by the hard nubs caused a physical response that was deliberate and tailored for his physique. Like the chemicals coursing through his veins and saturating his organs, they were a precision treatment. The gravity increased even more, doubling what was already doubled, and yet he lived. Blood didn't pool in the extremities, cells within the blood did not rupture, the heart didn't stop pumping. His vision didn't blur and darken until he sank into blissful unconsciousness and death.

No, far from it. That would be too merciful. Alan felt his pupils constrict. The medics told him that feeling was imagination, and explained the physiological response of a human body under immense gravitational strain while being flooded with stimulants. He couldn't recall what they said. Words were too heavy to hold onto. He felt a tightening and a tearing, from within his eyeball, as if an aperture were grinding closed. It felt real enough, even sounded real enough, despite what the medics thought. A small section of the bulkhead above him became exceptionally clear, so focused he could not take his eyes off it. Nor would he. He was trapped for the eight hours of acceleration. Eight hours, followed by the total release of gravity where he could recover a sense of self before the next acceleration, and the next, as the ship increased in speed, and sped even faster towards the sun.

Until then, he stared at the small area of bulkhead above him. Numbed to all physical pain, he dug up his own, reached deep inside and placed her face in the middle of his vision. He knew she would come. Pretending to die, memorizing muscle groups, focused vision—it didn't matter. This time, she would ride with him.

He thought he was over it, and he mostly was, but that kind of pain was slow to fade. He even called her before he left. She had a hesitancy in her voice, and he noticed it.

"I'm leaving in a couple days," he said. "Just wondering if you wanted to have a drink or something?"

Or something. He should have left that out. He hoped she would, and hoped it might lead to a gentle farewell, but in that instant of hesitancy he knew it wouldn't.

"I'd love to," she answered, relief evident in her voice. "But I'm in D.C. right now. I took a post at the university."

She almost let herself go. Only in hindsight could he hear the clip at the end of her gasp. The short breath as she tried to inhale the two words back in. Her mouth was near his ear, her breath quick and shallow. Sweat dripped from his head, joining hers and soaking the sheets. Her fingertips dug into his back. She liked his back, she told him, she liked feeling the muscles, liked wrapping her limbs around it.

"My man," she said between breaths. Or as a breath. He smiled when she said it. He wanted to be her man, wanted her to let him.

He tried to remember what happened next, but could only recall the feeling, the warmth and satisfaction of her words. They touched him and warmed him from the center of his heart. Their slow dance continued, only now much closer. Not physically—that was close from the beginning, passionate and sweaty and healing and safe because that was what it mostly was. But her two words meant part of the wall around her was being removed.

He rolled off her and licked the sweat around her nipples and under her breasts. She let him finish when he wanted, no matter how long he wanted to take, just as long he finished her after. Working his way down, he reached the smooth-shaven skin of her pubis mons and her waiting center.

"Do you like it?" she asked shortly after their first night together, drying after a shower, standing behind her, hands against her flat stomach, both gazing at each other in the mirror. He bent his knees and positioned his stiffening cock between her ass cheeks in answer. He added, "Yes, very much," in case she held any doubt.

Her fingers gripped his hair as she climaxed, finishing in a way that needed little training on her part. He knew what she wanted ("Hard around the nipples, gentle down there," was all she said the first time he explored). His hand stroked himself as he licked, and as her back arched in climax he moved up and entered her, beginning their rhythmic dance again, an energetic exercise. They soaked the sheets more, bedding she never washed once during the month of their affair.

He wanted to hear her say it again. He held her wet body against his, his ear near her mouth, waiting. But she didn't.

He saw her words now as a window rather than a wall, an opening into a raw and vulnerable place that was quickly closed again. It took a while to notice, brief moments of lucidity when the fugue of sex and lust cleared, just enough to catch a glimpse. Images came easier than words when thinking about her. Falling through the vacuum of space as metaphor for falling in love. He liked that one. Falling is usually associated with landing, painfully, which is why people are scared to fall, even if it is for love. But he saw what he felt at the time, and what he thought she felt, more as freefall—a type of floating with no reference. It took courage to fall that way, to admit there is no place to land, only descent.

Live and without the aid of a safety net, falling forever.

He turned onto his back, reached over and lifted the glass of water waiting there. Handing it to her, she gulped half and handed it back. She rose from the bed and he watched her walk out of the room and to the bathroom down the hall. He heard the shower.

"My man," she said. But only the once.

And again, not just in hindsight, he noticed, or heard, subtle messages, so subtle he wasn't even sure she noticed them herself. At 'whiskey time' one evening he finally brought up the feelings that were aching to be said. They sat on the bank of the river at sunset, passing a flask between them, an evening tipple in continuation of a tradition her father passed down from his father. The whiskey was smooth, an expensive label from Scotland, his contribution to the drinks shelf.

"I have this picture," he began. Pictures were the only way he could articulate, the words demanding visualization.

She looked over, with an expression less than enthusiastic. He remembered her mentioning a previous relationship, how unhappy she became, and how one morning she left without ever talking to the man, without ever explaining. He didn't want to be that guy, so he pressed on.

"It's like we were falling, like you do in space, with no gravity," he said. "You don't really fall; it just seems that way. There's no reference, no ground. It can be terrifying. Or it can be exhilarating, liberating."

She took a sip from the flask. He wanted to ask her if she understood, was she following? She only replied by handing back the flask.

"I feel like that's what we've been doing," he said instead. "Falling." In love, he wanted to add, but didn't because on a deeper level, one he didn't let himself see, it was already too late.

"Only it feels like instead of falling now, we've found a kind of ledge and are sitting on it," he said. "And I don't really understand why."

She shifted. He wasn't sure if it was to face him better, or to move away.

"I ..." she started. "I don't feel it anymore."

"What does that mean?" he asked.

"It just isn't there," she said.

"I still don't know what you're saying," he said, though he began to feel a hand closing around his heart.

"It's just ..." she reached over, took the flask and sipped slowly, staring at the river. "It was really nice in the beginning, beautiful, but now it ... I don't feel that anymore."

He watched the words float between them, not falling anywhere. "Like you just woke up and felt differently?" he asked, trying to say it without sarcasm or accusation. She didn't seem to notice if he failed.

"Yeah," she said, still watching the river. "Like that."

"Everything just happened so quicky," she added.

The hand around his heart squeezed tighter, dug in its claws. Questions and arguments raced through his mind. Anything to change her mind. Make her feel 'it' again. But he knew nothing he could do or say would do that.

He gazed at her profile, blonde hair partially covering her tanned face. She reached over and placed her hand on top of his.

"You are very special," she said.

He stayed at her place two more days, and they made love each night, though not as passionately as before, more as a courtesy to each other, a wordless farewell. He decided farewell sex was the worst type, where he wanted to hold on tight when it was actually a form of letting go. She drove him to the station when it was time, and she cried when they parted, letting the tears run freely down her cheeks.

He never understood those tears.

2

Alan watched as the spot on the ceiling shifted, the narrow scope of his focus sliding across the smooth surface of the metal. Her face slipped out of view as the chair tilted and he let it. Would the psychologists call that 'imaginary pain'? It felt real enough at the time, heart break or heart ache, disappointment, rejection, loneliness, even fear ... they hurt all the same. Sure, it felt different now. Time did that. Lessened the pain, if not entirely healed the wound. Maybe that was a good thing, never completely being over it, all those many little wounds acquired simply through being alive and feeling. He would smile, sitting in the acceleration couch under the weight of eight gravities, if it didn't require so much effort.

The chair stopped tilting and his feet elevated above his heart. Every two hours of acceleration it tilted forward or it tilted back, ensuring his chemically infused blood continued to circulate rather than pool in any extremities. The human body was not designed to be subjected to eight times the gravity of Earth for hours on end, so the aerospace engineers and the biomedical chemists made it possible. Nobs continued to poke and prod, physically stimulating his flesh, while electrical pulses reacted with the fluids injected into his body. But the scientists were kind. Alan didn't physically feel a thing, except what he dredged up from within his mind. He watched the small section of ceiling, as thousands of kilometers passed with every second the ship accelerated.

Speed was important, he understood that. Kind of. The math and the physics were well beyond his comprehension. Speed enabled the absorption of photons at an increased rate, so that enough power could be generated to create a gravity well large enough to slip through a small rip in the fabric of space and time. It was more a fold than a rip, but tears or holes were easier to visualize. Alan didn't have to understand the details. The ship was accelerating at great speed towards the sun, building up the power and momentum needed to create a wormhole to emerge in another time and place, and not within the sun itself.

He stared at the new section of ceiling. Her face was lost, so he brought up another. This was a bad idea. The experience was bad enough. Using pain to distract from discomfort was stupid, but his thoughts, as usual, had slipped their restraint and were wandering at will. Another face took shape. Cute button nose, skin peeling from too much sun. Thick glasses so she could see the world, glasses that he gently removed when they were not needed. Thick strawberry blonde hair. That was the color she told him when he asked. Did he make her feel the same way he felt that day, sitting beside the river, his heart being dissected? He didn't say he didn't feel it anymore, but he was young and he was foolish and he let her go, so she would forever remain a doubt and regret in his memory. Alan tried to remember the exact words he said, but couldn't. He remembered the look on her face, the smile fading when she realized what was happening. He hurt her, and he left her, taking a scholarship for doctoral studies in a different city

... best for them both, too hard to make it work ... those were some of the excuses.

Alan's vision blurred as a tear pooled before it careened down his cheek. She didn't cry that night. He hurt her, he broke her heart, he made a mistake. But she didn't cry. She was too good for that, too good for him. Alan tried to close his eyes but the stimulants didn't let him. He thought of what to say, if he could cross the years and had the opportunity. *I'm sorry? I made a mistake? If I had it all to do again ...?* All self-pitying and selfish thoughts, whose sole purpose would be to make him feel better. He caused her pain, so all he could do now was feel a small bit of it. He was the one who was afraid of falling that time. He left her, went to a new city, got a new apartment, started his new seminars, felt the emptiness and loneliness. He tried to call her several times, but not hard enough. It was already too late, a might have been, a what could have been, a what would never be.

Alan tasted the shame and it calmed him. His mind grew quiet, leaving aside the self-abuse as he did lists of muscle groups or lethal injections. And finally, thoughts became too heavy and he just stared at the sliver of ceiling, empty of everything except that small circle of awareness that shifted after a timeless period. When another needle pierced the skin on the inside of his arm, he realized that acceleration was over.

He tilted his head and watched clear fluid stream into his vein, replacing and negating the chemicals still in his system. His vision softened, the edges blurred and grew wide, foreground and background adjusting as his focus became clear. After several moments the needle retracted, exiting his skin and retreating into the chair. The mark inside his elbow stayed red, as it would for a long time, never given the chance to heal before being stabbed again.

Alan looked away, lifting his head slightly and following the motion around him. Jardin was rising, his wrinkled paper gown tearing as he stood, disintegrating in the wide circle of moisture at his waist. His briefs clearly burst. It happens. Jardin stood staring at his soiled body before gingerly stepping forward and walking out of the room. Alan glanced at his own waist and breathed out slowly. Small mercies. Sometimes they ruptured. Briefs. Incontinence pads. Whatever they were referred to, they were nothing but diapers for adults. The low-tech solution to a high-tech problem. No matter how cleaned out the body was prior to acceleration, there was always something more to be wrung out.

He moved his legs over the side of the chair until his feet touched the deck. He sat up, placing his hands on his thighs, each movement slow and controlled, resisting the urge to fight gravity. Despite the lightness he now felt, he had to remind himself that the force pinning him down for so long was gone, and only a trace remained. Stand too fast and he'd propel his body across the room, or into the ceiling. Gentle and slow, a new mantra. He placed what little weight there was on his feet and stood.

All the crew were up now, readjusting to their bodies just like Alan. Inessa, the captain, stood beside her chair and rubbed the inside of her elbow. Alan looked at the red mark on his own arm. A small bead of blood stood at the puncture wound. He wiped it away with a finger and stepped towards the exit, carefully placing a foot, shifting his weight, and lifting and moving the other, moving forward like a toddler learning to walk. His paper gown rustled at each step. At the recycler he grabbed it at the shoulder and pulled down, tearing the garment off and stuffing it into the receptacle. He sniffed his hand and smelled the hours of sweat and fear and regret. Pulling at the strips of tape at his waist he removed his diaper and made it similarly disappear.

Keeping his hands away from his face, he continued to the wash room. Steam lingered in the air as the filters struggled to suck it into the system. Alan pushed the hot water button and the air grew thicker as more steam filled the cubicle. Water cascaded over his body, flowed into the drain at his feet, circulated through filters and heated pipes and fell on him again in a closed loop. At least the water flowed downward, in the light gravity produced by the spin of the vessel. He opened his mouth and it filled. He gargled and spat on the floor, letting it circle through the system again. The image of Jardin walking away flashed through his mind and he spat again, followed by a laugh nobody heard. Everything they breathed, ate, and drank were recycled and shared. There was no place on board for squeamishness or modesty. Alan turned off the water, dried himself and put on a track suit before joining the others in the mess.

He took a seat at the table next to Jardin, who sat staring at the table. Alan poured a glass of water, downed it and poured another. Rehydration was important. Although all they did was lie in a chair, the beating of the intense gravitational force and drenching from the drugs left the body spent. Wasted. This time around the table was meant as a grounding, of sorts. A buffer between the hell of the chair, and a welcome sleep to come. It was initially filled with banter, when the first acceleration was finished. There was a sense of shared struggle, and shared ... survival. It was a time to vent.

"I hate acceleration," Thanh, the xeno-biologist said.

"You're supposed to," Ariana mumbled, her tongue trying to regain a sense of normality after hours pressed against the back of her mouth.

"My thoughts," Than carried on, ignoring her remark. "Thoughts I don't want, that won't go away ... I wish I could just pass out."

"If you lost consciousness, you'd never think again. You'd be dead," Ariana said.

"How fast do you think we're going?" Gunther de Hass, the Probe Controller, asked. It wasn't a question wanting an answer, more an escape of air.

"At least one hundred and twenty thousand kph," Dave Wise answered. "Next acceleration will double that." He looked like the others, pale with dark rings under the eyes. Beaten and exhausted. But this was the reactor technician's first trip so he was still excited. It would be different by his third time in the chair.

"I defecated and sat in my own shit for hours," Chen said, a comment designed to shut the reactor technician up.

"We all do at some time," Shu Len told him. She and the astrogator came from the same taikonaut program, and the same area of China. The medical officer was too nice to see that comment wasn't out of self-pity.

"And then double again," Dave said. "My God, to go so fast—"

"Shut up, Dave," Maria said. Coming from the first mate, it was an order rather than a wish. Dave lowered his eyes to the table like the others. By third acceleration he didn't need to be told. He felt like the others. He knew that the ship was going close to three hundred and eighty thousand kph, that after the fourth and last acceleration they would achieve half of a million kilometers per hour and acquired enough power to enter the sun, and exit three hundred light years away where the ship flipped and decelerated, eight hours at a time, until reaching their destination.

"Drink," Maria said again, and all understood it as order. She guided them by example, reaching out a tired hand, taking hold of the cup and lifting it to her lips. The others copied, even the captain.

"You know the drill," Inessa told her crew. "Rehydrate. Rest. Don't think about the next acceleration until it's time to prep. Sleep, a long, dark, dreamless sleep," she added.

Her Russian accent made it sound like a remedy handed down by her grandmother's grandmother. Alan tried to remember the word, *babushka*, but with his battered mind he couldn't. He smiled at her, her loose and damp blonde hair soon to be dried and plaited fiercely, her back soon to be straight again, after that long dark sleep. Now she looked as wrecked as the rest. He gazed around the table. It was a fruit basket of a crew. Russian, German, Chinese, Vietnamese. Maria, that Brazilian pilot. Ariana, the Italian co-pilot. Abede, the Senegalese xeno-botanist. Eva, the Czech xeno-linguist. Even an Argentinian. Alan nodded at Jardin, thought of clacking his glass as in toast, but decided it took too much effort. He and Dave were the only Americans, unlike the *Concurrent* mission, made up solely of American astronauts with military backgrounds.

Send a fruit basket out to visit the dead. Something for the civilians to do.

3

The first message took three months to decipher. It was clear from its very structure that it was different. It came at regular intervals and repeated itself. Both were features of the messages leaving earth. It meant the message was deliberate, sent with the intention to be heard. Sometimes that was all that was wanted. "Hello. We are here," was the gist of many sent from and heard by earthlings. But after three months of efforts to extract the information in the repeating pattern, three words were understood. Those three words contained in binary notation continued to repeat themselves for the remainder of the year, and then a little into the next. For thirteen months, a three-word message was broadcast from somewhere in the constellation Aquarius.

It said: "Message to follow."

The message that followed was the most complex ever received. It took fourteen hours to fully download, and almost an entire year to decode. Every university and observatory with the capacity to do so worked on the incredible quantity of data. Only when it was discovered by a graduate student at the Bern observatory that what she was looking at was not actually a message, but a lesson in linguistics, did the collective efforts start to pay off. The earth had been sent a Rosetta Stone in zeros and ones. The phonemes, digraphs, verbal conjugations and rules of grammar of an alien language were unlocked. At the end of the lesson were the three words already learned: "Message to follow."

In the third year, the Nyrians introduced themselves.

Humanity unwittingly reached out to the stars as soon as radio technology was created. Faint waves emanated from the planet, dispersing into the solar system and beyond at the speed of light. But if any trace of these signals were ever detected by an intelligent species on a distant world, they wouldn't be treated to the voice of Orson Wells describing an alien invasion, or re-runs of popular sitcoms, or the first televised transmission, that of Adolf Hitler announcing the beginning of the Berlin Olympics. Any electromagnetic signal would be degraded and consumed by the background static of the galaxy, mere radio waves leaking from the planet like drops of water from a saturated sponge.

Messages must be deliberate. Early efforts were physical, sent when crossing stellar distances relied solely on the ability to accelerate a craft through the vacuum of space. The Pioneer probe carried a plaque, engraved with the image a man and a woman, as well as a map of the solar system. Voyager brought with it a disc, which contained images, greetings in over fifty languages, and even music, including Louis Armstrong singing about what a wonderful world from which the craft originated. At its current velocity, Voyager will deliver that message to the nearest solar system in eighty thousand years.

Messages must be focused. In the year 2013 a brief note was sent to a red dwarf star located in the Boötes constellation named Gliese

526. It was a simple hailing, directions to the planet, an outline of the periodic table, and a definition of the hydrogen atom in binary code. It also directed any listener capable of deciphering it to a frequency where more messages existed. It was known as the Lone Signal Project, despite being many more than a single message. On that other frequency, messages of one hundred and forty-four characters were sent by anybody wishing to do so. The first message was free, but additional shouts into space cost a small fee. The Lone Signal Project shut down shortly after transmission began due to lack of funding.

Gliese 526 is seventeen light years from Earth, so the communication would not reach any exo-planet there for over seventeen years, and the reply, if any, another seventeen years to return to earth. It was a shot in the dark, that depended on ears to hear it (a species with the technological ability to detect the physical phenomenon of the message) and the intellectual sophistication to perceive the information (a species with the sentience to comprehend it). Those behind the Lone Signal Project didn't stick around to wait for a response, moving on to other projects or schemes once they quickly went bankrupt. Their dream of a chain of satellite dishes across the globe beaming messages into space remained unfulfilled. In 2030, thirty-four years after the earth reached out, no response from Gliese 526 was detected by scientists keeping up an active search for extra-terrestrial life.

Proponents of METI (Messaging Extra-Terrestrial Life), like those behind the Lone Signal Project, shouted into the skies. It was a controversial approach, but done because ... it could be done. In 1974, a message was transmitted from the Arecibo radio telescope in Puerto Rico towards the M13 globular cluster, located over twenty-four thousand lightyears away. Nobody was planning on sticking around for the required forty-eight thousand years to listen for a response. The message celebrated the reopening of the telescope, and was sent just because it could. With the technology of the day, the message continued to degrade as it traveled and never reach its target. But it was a celebration. As technology improved, so too did the messaging.

Not all were happy with this. Some asked, quite reasonably, whether it was safe to shout into a dark room, not knowing what was inside it. Any species with the technological ability to both listen to an informal invitation and then show up was certainly more advanced than humanity at that time. It was a science fiction trope, but a legitimate worry. The earth had been invaded many times, watched by millions, albeit on the silver screen. With imagination so vivid, the lack of response was desired. Others tried to explain the cosmic silence differently. The Zoo Hypothesis maintained that the silence was deliberate avoidance. As if a large sign stood near the exhibit: "Don't feed the animals." Others held that extra-terrestrial life was more benevolent, trying to prevent any interplanetary contamination. Or, as the Laboratory Hypothesis held, earth *was* the experiment. Just like sticking a finger in a petri dish, contact might contaminate results. Or, again hoping for benevolence, *they* simply were waiting until humanity reached a certain level of development, technologically, or morally.

It was all fantasy. The galaxy was big, and the space between stars immense, measured not by distance, but time. The time it took light to travel from one point to another. But even that time was not the same. Light from Gliese 526 reaching the earth was seventeen years old by the time it reached the planet. What was actually seen was a glimpse into the past. Chances were very good that a civilization on a planet in the globular cluster known as M13 may not even exist in forty-eight thousand years, once any listeners responded. With humanity's propensity towards conflict, it was valid to worry if it would even last another fifty, or one hundred years. The Fermi Paradox maintained that the time between civilizations was just too great for two civilizations to ever meet. Even if an alien civilization existed one hundred thousand, ten thousand, or even a mere thousand years in the past, that was enough to never meet.

But dedicated listeners maintained their vigil. Satellites searched the heavens, from the planet, and in orbit. Scientists listened to distant radio waves and heard echoes made mere micro seconds after the Big Bang. As the ability to listen grew, humanity heard more, from closer to home, and within our own galaxy. By the time the first deliberate message was received and deciphered, humanity even had the technology to render distance, and time, irrelevant.

4

Alan entered the auditorium. It was too large for purpose, reminding him more of a university lecture hall than a space agency briefing room. He made his way down the stairs, saw an empty seat in one of the first rows, and stopped.

"This free?" he asked, indicating to the chair.

"Not free at all, sir," a man with a military grade haircut answered. "That seat cost years of service. Why don't you grab one in back with the Fly Buys?"

It took a moment for Alan's mind to recognize ridicule or insult. When it finally did, he looked at his open hand and wondered who was more fortunate that he wasn't the type of man to strike out in such moments. A punch or a slap would have been satisfying, but Alan knew that he was the lucky one that day. A moment of satisfaction would no doubt have cost his seat on the mission. He opened his hand instead and raised it to his forehead in a mock salute.

"Roger that, commodore," Alan said.

"It's Lieutenant Commander Lawson," Lieutenant Commander Lawson replied.

"Of course, it is," Alan said, lowering his hand and beginning to walk away. "Says so right there on your flight suit."

Alan went up two levels and made his way to the middle row where a dark-haired man sat. He took the seat next to him and laughed. "Good to see you again, Jardin," Alan said, patting the other's leg.

"What was that about?" Jardin asked, indicating the officer sitting below them.

"Just playing with him," Alan confessed. "Captain America didn't want to sit next to me."

"Don't be disheartened, my friend," Jardin said. "You are just wearing the wrong clothes. I will find you a costume shop and then you will fit right in."

"Nah. I never liked uniforms. I'll just slum it with you," Alan said. He leaned over Jardin and gave the man next to him his hand. "Alan Reading," he said. "Atmospheric Science."

"Dave Wise, Reactor Technician."

"Canadian?" Alan asked.

"Minnesota," Dave said. "Bemidji."

"Never heard of it," Alan said. "California," he added, pointed a thumb at his chest.

"See, you don't need a uniform after all," Jardin said. "You have your own American club now."

"Fair to say we're not welcome in that," Alan said. "Have to work with the riff raff, eh, Dave of Bemidji?"

The reactor technician didn't have time to reply. The three grew quiet as an older man walked onto the stage below. He stepped to a podium and looked at the two dozen men and women in his audience. They all knew who he was, worked with him on previous missions, or met him at an interview to be able to sit in the room they were now in. But he would still introduce himself as he always did.

"My name is Doctor Henry Moreno," he said. "And it is my great pleasure to stand before you and represent not only the International Space Agency, but lead the Interstellar *Response* Program. I believe, as I am sure you do, that the work we do is of the utmost importance for humanity as we continue to reach across the expanse, with our hand extended, to those who have made the effort to reach out to us." At this point Doctor Moreno extended his own hand towards those below him as he segued into platitudes and responsibilities.

"You, sitting here today, are the hand of humanity. We reach out through you. But you are so much more. You are our eyes, and mind, and heart." Doctor Moreno placed a hand over his own heart, breathed deeply, and continued.

"Same speech as last time," Alan whispered.

"Indeed, it is," Jardin agreed.

Alan leaned over the Argentine to speak to the American. "Pretty exciting stuff, eh?" he asked Dave. "It's going to be a few minutes' history, followed by the crucial importance of the present mission, then et cetera et cetera et cetera."

"It is exciting," Dave said.

"Exciting times," Alan agreed, sitting back in his chair. "I see Eva is back for more."

"Yes, she is," Jardin said. "Along with her talented tongue."

"More of a talented ear," Alan said. "She is a linguist. Most of that is just about being able to listen. Wait, here come the introductions."

"... So, I would like to now bring to the stage the two who will carry the burden and responsibility of leadership for the coming missions. Captain Todd Nichols of the *Solar Flare*, and Captain Inessa Volkov, of the *Sunspot*. Please, a round of applause for the leaders of our *Con-*

current and *Response* ships." Moreno clapped his hands as twenty-two others joined him. A lanky man in a crisp uniform stood in the first row and made his way towards the stage. Several rows up a woman rose. She laughed briefly at something the person next to her said, her blond hair waving as she nodded her head. She brushed off her dress, removing invisible creases. Alan smiled as she walked down to the stage.

"Look at your face, my friend," Jardin said. "You are in love."

"Everybody's in love with Inessa," Alan answered. "She's our captain."

Moreno continued to talk, but Alan tuned out the words and watched the woman on stage. She chose a floral print dress that ended just below her knees, and flat soled sandals. Alan thought she looked like a Russian summer day, though he had never been to the Federation in any season. She smiled and nodded, laughing briefly at something Nichols said. He, in turn laughed at her response. She was the antithesis of the military man, at least in outward appearance. Her choice of attire was deliberate, her views about military in *Response* or *Concurrent* missions well known, and beneath the smiles and laughs they were engaged in a discussion started years ago.

Captain Inessa Volkov descended the stage and the crew of the *Sunspot* began to rise. Alan snapped out of his day dream when Jardin rose to join them. He followed the group into an adjacent briefing room where they took their places around an oval table. Inessa smiled at them.

"Let us join hands," she said, opening hers. The two on either side took them and the others joined the chain. Most smiled as they did so, but the two new team members looked confused.

"I am so happy to see you all again, and to embark on another mission as your captain," she said.

Dave looked at his hands, and then at Inessa. She met his eyes.

"I want to welcome two to our family," she said. "David Wise from the United States, and Thanh Goa from the Socialist Republic of Vietnam." She turned and smiled at the thin man on her left. "Dave is our reactor technician. He has transferred from NASA, where he worked in development. We are very lucky to have him on board. He brings very valuable experience. Dave, welcome."

"Thank you," Dave said. His hands felt sweaty and trapped.

"Thanh comes directly from the Vietnam National Space Center and the University of Hanoi, where he is a professor of xeno-biology. Thanh, I hope your research will be fruitful." She nodded at him, and looked around the table.

"Such a good crew," she said. "I am truly lucky."

"You chose us all," Abede said. "There is no luck involved."

"That is true," Inessa said. "I chose each and every one of you. I would not want to cross space with any other."

She opened her hands and they let go of each other. Dave wiped his palms on his trousers.

"In another room there is a banquet waiting," Inessa said. "Food and drink, wine and beer. Visit with the crew of the *Solar Flare*. Play nice. Their egos are fragile, and their bravado is just a mask.

"And if you imbibe," she continued, "do so moderately. It will be the last alcohol you will drink until the mission is complete. Training and preparations begin tomorrow and we will have to take off our pretty dresses and become very serious about our duties. Most of you already know this, so I am saying it for Thanh and Dave. Some of what you are going to experience will mostly be ... rather unpleasant."

She stopped as laughter rippled around the table. "I know, that is maybe not the right adjective. But everything you experience will be rewarded. Everything will be worth it, when you see another world. They have reached out, they have sent an invitation, and we ..."

Inessa looked at each of her crew, her smile closer to a grin. "And we are going to see who they were. We will be humanity's reconnaissance. What we find may lead to the first meeting between species."

"It was a Czech, wasn't it?" Alan asked. He swigged from a bottle of beer as he stood beside the linguist. "That cracked the code?"

"She was Swiss," Eva replied.

"Swiss, Czech, not the same thing?"

"Don't pretend to be stupid, you're good enough at it already."

Alan took another drink. He knew he would have too many and pay for it in the morning, but he wouldn't be the only one. And he didn't really care.

"And it wasn't a code," Eva added. "It was binary. Very complicated mathematics boiled down to two digits."

"Zeros and ones," Alan said. "What else do you need? She was into the I Ching or something, wasn't she?"

"Daoist, I think."

"Yin and yang, zero and one. I can see that," Alan said.

"Sure, you can," Eva said. "The first message took three months to decipher and you can see that. She was brilliant. Even if it was an accident."

"The bagua meets the qubit," Alan said. "Our distant friends are very smart."

"Let's hope. And you're not as dumb as you look," Eva said. "What are you doing?"

"What do you mean?"

"Right now. With me," Eva said.

"Just flirting," Alan said. "It's good to see you again. All of you."

"You sound like you missed us."

"I did," Alan admitted. He looked at the table holding drinks and at the empty bottle in his hand.

"That's sad, my friend," Eva said.

"It is indeed."

"Get another beer and tell me about it," Eva said.

"Just the beer," Alan said. "I'm not really ready for that kind of talk."

"Why don't you go and mingle with your countrymen then?" Eva asked.

"That place bruised me," Alan said. "Beat me to a bloody pulp. I'll leave the mingling to our new crew member. He's from somewhere in the mid-west. They're a friendly lot out there."

Eva stared at him. "What was her name?" she asked.

Alan laughed and shook his head.

"Offer's there if you want an ear," Eva said. "You don't have the best track record with women. Maybe talking with one you're not romantically entangled with would be helpful."

"Just the beer for now," Alan said. He briefly placed a hand on her shoulder before heading to the drinks table. "But thanks."

"Maybe later then," Eva said.

Alan laughed. "Message to follow," he said.

He watched his captain talk to her counterpart and two crew from the *Concurrent* mission and didn't notice the Brazilian pilot stand beside him.

"—I said, pour me a red." Maria poked him in the ribs. "And quit staring and just go and talk to them."

"Why does everybody think I need to be with the Americans?" he asked, filling a glass with a merlot. He regretted his tone as soon as it was out.

"Sorry," Maria said, raising her palms. She lowered a hand and accepted the glass.

"They don't even think we're necessary," he said. "They call us the Fly Buys; did you know that? Like we just bought a ticket, take a little tour, and go back home. They think a probe could be sent instead, save money."

"But then the international community would have nothing to do," Maria added. "Nothing to show for their support. Let us go see the ghosts, take pictures of the dead."

"Wow. I thought I was jaded," Alan said.

"I am not jaded," Maria replied. "I am blessed. I will, as our beautiful captain says, visit a new world."

"I'll drink to that." Alan gently touched Maria's wine glass with the neck of his beer bottle.

"HIP-3451 was wonderful. So busy, so many people. They were an amazing civilization," Maria said.

"But *Concurrent* found a dead planet," Alan added. "They poisoned themselves."

"That is not relevant," Maria argued. "What we saw was real, and it was alive when we were there. We did not visit the dead. They did." Maria indicated to the *Concurrent* crew with her half-filled glass.

"That whole planet is dead now," Alan said.

"You're depressing me. Stop it," Maria said. "Everything will die someday. Even humanity." She took another sip of wine. "But that doesn't matter anymore. Time doesn't matter anymore. We're not the ones visiting ghosts. They asked us to come. They didn't just send a message; they sent an invitation. That's a new one. We get to see who they are. Your countrymen don't know who or what they will find. Can't you see it?" she asked.

"See what?"

"Them, looking at us," she said. "They're jealous. They want to be us."

Alan followed her gaze. "That's a nice thought."

"It's the truth." She set her empty glass on the table and shook her head when Alan indicated the wine bottle. "You'd better call it quits with those two," she said, watching Alan open another beer.

"I'll pay for it tomorrow," he said.

"That you most certainly will."

"Maria?"

"Yes?"

"Thank you," Alan said.

"What did I do now?" she asked.

Alan smiled at her, at a loss for words. She stepped forward, hugged him and kissed his cheek. "You're with your family now. Celebrate with us," she said. "We're about to do something amazing."

Alan reached for another beer and saw Inessa across the room, in a discussion with Nichols. She wore a smile her crew knew well, which politely told whomever she was speaking with that she was right, they were mistaken, and they would realize that eventually. Alan winced as he remembered an occasion when she smiled like that at him on his first mission. Inessa stopped talking, caught his eye, bent a finger and motioned him over. He took a bottle and opened it before walking to the small group.

"This is our atmospheric specialist, Alan Reading," she said, taking Alan's arm and moving him closer to the group. "He is a countryman of yours, from California."

The captain offered his hand, and firmly shook Alan's. "California," he said, "north or south?"

"North," Alan said. "Sacramento."

"The River City," Nichols said. "I know it well. I started flying out of McAndrew's when I first got my wings, a very long time ago. Good bars in Old Town."

"I'll agree with you on that, Captain," Alan said.

"Please, call me Todd." He indicated to the two next to him. "Let me introduce Dana, our communications specialist, and Sam, our probe controller."

Alan felt gripped by the communication specialist's green eyes. She took his hand and shook, firm but polite. She wore a tailored white blouse with epaulets on her shoulders and dark blue slacks. Alan smiled and slightly adjusted his position to uniforms, at least on some. He reluctantly let go of her hand and took the probe controller's, who gripped it as if trying to prove something.

"Alan is among the most experienced of our crew. This will be his fourth mission with the *Response* team," Inessa said.

"What was your last assignment?" Todd asked.

"HIP," he answered.

"That was a very sad trip," Dana said. "I felt so useless."

"You couldn't have known what you would find," Alan said.

"That is what makes each mission so difficult," she said. "You, on the other hand, know there will be life. You are so blessed."

"That is exactly how a crewmate just described it," Alan said.

"It's true," Dana agreed.

"We don't have a communication specialist on the *Sunspot*," Alan said. "Our xeno-linguist doubles in that role. How does your work differ from the xeno-linguist?"

"Languages change, as do means of communication," Dana said. "Just look at how English has changed over the centuries. You respond to a message, so you know a language that is being used. The linguist has that to work with. When we intercept communications on a target planet, hundreds or thousands of years may have passed. Languages change. Technology changes."

"And our very brilliant communication specialist figures out how to make sense of what we hear," Todd said. "She was on the team that developed the translator devices."

"Impressive," Inessa said.

Alan felt the probe controller's eyes on him. He took a swig from his beer and tried to ignore it, but not successfully. He turned and met the man's gaze, trying not to classify a person he barely knew in the same category as that son of a bitch Lawson he met earlier.

"And you," Sam asked. "How do you describe it?"

"Excuse me?" Alan asked.

"Your mission. *Response*," Sam said.

Alan smiled. "When we arrive at the target, after suffering acceleration, after suffering deceleration, I feel like the luckiest man alive."

"I think that describes us all," the *Concurrent* captain said. "Luckiest *people*," he corrected, nodding towards Inessa and Dana. He shot his probe controller a glance before returning his attention to Inessa. "The smell of coffee and the sight of that cake is proving too tempting," he said. "Any objections to moving to the dessert table?"

"No objections at all," Inessa answered.

"I'll have to make my way to quarters soon," Alan said. "Tomorrow will probably be as taxing as acceleration. Todd, Dana, Sam, it's been a pleasure to meet you. I wish you success in your mission."

"And you, Alan," Captain Todd Nichols replied, firmly shaking Alan's hand again, before leading the party away.

5

Chen and Shu Len sat together at the table, sipping what smelled like beef broth. The astrogator's hair was flattened on one side of his head and stuck out on the other as if it were trying to escape. His eyes were puffy and red, but his face relaxed. Shu Len smiled and shook her head at something he said. They switched to English, lingua franca of the ship, as soon as Alan entered. It was a polite gesture. They wore the same track suit as he, grey bottoms and grey long sleeve top, the only color on it an orange sunburst with the name *Sunspot* below it. Alan padded to the coffee machine in one of his few non-regulation possessions, a pair of sheepskin slippers. One small comfort from home. Most kept their items private. A special book, a photograph, a piece of jewelry. Alan went for unsentimental comfort, at least for his feet. He packed a special memento—a book of poetry, and just like the others, kept it very private.

He breathed in the aroma of the coffee before taking a sip. Chen and Shu Len went back to whispered Cantonese. One by one other crew joined the table, their long rest over. Jardin took a seat next to

Alan, put his arms on the table and laid his head on them. Alan patted Jardin's shoulder, then rubbed the Argentine's back before returning to his drink. Dave walked straight to the coffee machine, dialed a mug, took it when it was filled and sat at the table staring at it. Thanh entered and sat next to him, staring at his hands.

"That's how we must have looked on our first trip," Alan said quietly to Jardin.

"That *was* how we looked," Jardin agreed. "Poor *chiquitos* still don't know what is going to hit them."

"I don't even want to think about it," Alan said. "I just want to enjoy this coffee."

Inessa emerged from the galley, followed by Gunther, both carrying large trays. They set them on the table and started passing around plates, each filled with pastries. The captain then filled any mugs needing a top up. She touched each crew member as she did so and said a few words, beginning with the new crew.

"Did you dream?" she asked Thanh. "I always dream of home during that sleep. Of our dacha by the lake. It is a calm, clear morning in my dream, and the water like a mirror."

"I …" Thanh started. "No, I just slept," he finished.

"That is good," Inessa said. "Deep, dark sleep. You look much refreshed."

She turned to Dave, her hand resting on his shoulder. "Good morning, Dave."

"Good morning, Inessa," he answered, looking up. His eyes met hers and he couldn't help but mirror her smile.

"It is a good morning," she said before moving around the table.

"Gunther has made his *worlds* famous cinnamon and raison swirls," she added, "to celebrate this new day. I want you to enjoy them. They come all the way from Dusseldorf—"

"*Aus Solingen, miene kapitan*," Gunther corrected her.

"—from Solingen, in the west of Germany. I am told they are made from a secret family recipe. What a fortunate family. This morning they are shared with our family, as is tradition on the *Sunspot*." Inessa took the only empty chair, picked up a pastry and took a bite. She wiped icing from her lip with a finger and licked it. "These are so good," she said. "Gunther, the culinary world's loss is our gain."

"*Danke, meine—*"

"Stop it, Gunther," Inessa said. "Dave, Thanh, I will not lie to you. This will be the nicest breakfast pastry you will eat in your life. The coffee in front of you will be the nicest you will ever drink."

She closed her eyes and took a sip from her mug, and held the drink in front of her meditatively. The others waited for her to speak, but gave up one at a time and began to eat their pastry. Dave and Thanh glanced at the others, unable to conceal their anxiety. Eva indicated to their pastries and they both picked theirs up at the same time. Thanh let out a nervous giggle and Dave joined him.

"This is really good, Gunther," Dave said.

Gunther merely smiled at Dave and continued to eat. Dave accepted the silence as part of the ... he wasn't sure what their breakfast party was. Another tradition? The captain gave Dave a wink, before going back to making love to her coffee. Abede licked icing off his fingers, nothing but crumbs left of his German treat. But he, too, remained silent. Dave remembered church as teenager, the time after holy communion, back at his pew, the bland wafer melting in his mouth, all around him silent until the ceremony was complete. That was what this was, he realized. A ceremony. He took another bite and washed it down with coffee, waiting for the reason to be revealed.

When all the pastries had been eaten and coffees refilled, Jardin broke the silence. "Gunther's pastry is a spiral," he observed.

Nobody contradicted him. Dave and Thanh exchanged glances, and then listened with the others.

Jardin made a circular motion with his finger, tracing smaller circles until the point of his finger remained motionless in the center of his circles.

"We spiral and acquire energy, absorbing the sun's power, until we use it for our own purpose," he said. "That is my role on the *Sunspot*. It is my responsibility. I fold time and space. To others, that might sound like ego, but you know different. You know it is humility. My calculations will create a gravity well that lets us move across space as if distance did not exist. My calculations will warp the time continuum and place us *when* we chose to be." He swallowed, took a long moment to blink, and breathed out. "If I fail, we will all die. You will all die. I promise it will be quick, and that you will not feel a thing."

Jardin smiled at the group. "But I want you to know that I love you, and if we disintegrate in the sun, I am sorry. I won't have a chance to say that later, so I say it now. I am sorry."

"Not going to happen," Chen said.

"I don't accept," Ariana protested. "Just do your job."

"No way," Alan added. "I'll see you on the other side."

"There is no need to apologize, my friend," Abede said. "It has been an honor to know you."

"Abede!" Eva said. "He isn't going to kill us."

"But he might," Abede countered.

"We will assume that he will not," Inessa said. "In fact, we will ensure his success by letting him work. The rest of us have preparations to make. It is two days until acceleration and the event, followed by a hard deceleration. I want all equipment checked. As soon as our science team have done so with their own equipment, they will assist Gunther in the flight bay, and Dave at the reactor. Two with each. In the next twenty-four hours I want each of you to visit Shu Len for a complete physical. She will begin administering the pre-grav regimen when you see her."

Inessa looked down the table. "Dave, you will see Shu Len first. That way you'll have uninterrupted time to focus on your machine."

6

"Your heart rate is a little elevated, but your pressure is fine," Shu Len said.

"It's usually on the low side," Dave answered.

"I know, I'm your doctor."

She handed him a vial and he spat into it before handing it back. Shu Len inserted it into a centrifuge and they watched it spin for a moment before reading the monitor next to it. Data scrolled across the screen. To Dave they were meaningless numbers.

"So far so good," Shu Len said. "Now the blood."

He offered an arm and she inserted a needle, attached a small vile and when it was full of blood inserted it into the centrifuge. She nodded at the results.

"Good to go," she said. "Just relax. Focus on your work, and not the crossing. There's nothing to be done about that."

"Is it twice as bad?" he asked.

"Twice as ... There's nothing to be done about it." Shu Len washed her hands, dried them and dropped the towel in the recycler. "And you know exactly what is happening. Focus on your work. It's your reactor."

"I understand that. But knowing is different from experiencing," Dave said. He got up to leave the small sickbay, stopped at the door and turned. "And tell me, why was that the nicest breakfast pastry I will ever eat in my life? I mean, it was good, but, well ..."

"I can give you something to help relax now if you need it, there's enough time for it to clear your system," she answered.

"I'm just asking," Dave said.

"Okay," Shu Len answered. "When we're in the chair, and the mind won't let go, if you are lucky, you might remember a certain German treat. You will see its white frosting, the swirl of its pastry, the raisins hidden within. You will smell it, fresh out of the oven. Its intoxicating aroma will fill you. And you will remember the taste, that first moment it touched your tongue. You will think of that pastry, hopefully, and not anything else. It will fill that small space on the ceiling you are focusing on. It, and nothing or nobody else. That is the hope, anyway."

"I think I get it."

"You don't, not quite yet," she said. "But you will later. And we're done now, so off to work."

"Thanks," he said as he left.

"Don't thank me, thank Gunther. And send Ariana, please."

Thanh and Alan assisted at the reactor, processing a seemingly endless list of checks. The mechanics of the engine were far outside their fields of expertise, but they could read lights and scroll through data, which freed the reactor technician to tend to more delicate matters. Despite being in the largest room in the ship, the scientists were confined to an array of monitors in the control cubicle. Dave moved about the fission reactor, joined by Jardin from time to time, who conferred silently before returning to his own work.

The remaining hours were punctuated by mealtimes and rest periods, both skipped by most. As the time neared, each took the purgative administered by Shu Len, and the regimen of pre-acceleration medications. Each donned their paper gowns and mounted their chairs in silence, numbed by the thought of the hours of gravity facing them and by the chemicals beginning to circulate through their bodies. Alan sat in his chair staring at the ceiling as the needle pricked his arm. He felt the warm fluid enter his body and waited for the world to narrow, not trying to divert his mind with games or even memories. He simply waited for the images that would come. The pastry was delicious, but it never helped him.

The chair tilted and he sank into the gel. Mechanical knuckles prodded and probed. The small section of ceiling, the limit of his focus, shifted, and then shifted again as the hours progressed. Then the weight lifted. All weight lifted. For the briefest of moments, there was relief, respite from the oppression of gravity. Alan sighed as his body lifted against the chair's restraining straps. He waiting for death, or worse. The *Sunspot* entered the corona of the sun, and fell into the space between stars, between times, between life and death. Alan felt his mind fold backwards, arching until it formed a circle, a sphere, that collapsed until it became a single speck of darkness that grew dimmer and dimmer. And just before it disappeared, just before it detonated into a blinding explosion, he slammed down into his chair and the weight of eight planets crushed his chest. Somewhere in his mind he knew the ship had crossed over, that Jardin's calculations were flawless, and they were now three hundred lightyears from earth, three hundred years in the past, thrown towards a new world. The intense pressure he felt was generated by the same force that propelled them at the sun, only now it acted to slow their momentum.

For eight more hours he stared at a small section of the ceiling ... and faces and memories continued to fill them, his past playing out. The first time he remembered feeling shame, feeling regret. The people he hurt. The people who hurt him. Re-played and re-watched, sitting in a cinema with no exit except when the weight crushing him was too much even for memory. Shu Len had a long explanation for what the chemicals did to his conscious mind in order to keep him conscious.

"A cinnamon and raison scroll would probably put you to sleep," she told him. "That's why you never call it up. You need more."

"Sleep isn't bad," he answered.

"When we are under acceleration or deceleration, sleep will lead to death," she said. "You know that. You are fortunate. Your memories, and the feelings you describe as so real, they keep you alive."

"Then why bother with the breakfast?"

"Not every mind works like yours, thank goodness," Shu Len said.

"They make me long for sleep," Alan admitted.

The spot on the ceiling narrowed and a familiar face filled it. She smiled at him, as she had smiled before, an expression of sadness adding beauty to her tanned face. Alan knew she would be replaced by a button nose and strawberry blond hair. And she would be followed by ... Alan gave into the past. The spot on the ceiling shifted, and shifted again. He saw the chest of drawers and relived a moment. It wasn't his finest. She was at work, he at home on a sick day. It was their third year together, a relationship started as he finished his studies. They moved in, started their careers and their lives together. But passion turned to routine turned to whatever it turns into. Alan suspected she was seeing someone. He saw the obvious signs and ignored them to the best of his abilities.

Until that morning. He opened one drawer, and then the next. He opened her underwear drawer, feeling like the intruder he was. He pushed some lacy garments aside and saw it, an unsealed envelope. He lifted it out, opened the envelope and withdrew a letter. He began to read. No, not his finest moment. It was to her lover. He didn't remember the words. He saw them through a film of salty water. Words of promise, words of commitment, words of desire. Alan watched the ceiling helplessly, watched as he refolded the letter, placed it back in its envelope, and then in its hiding place. He closed the drawer and left the room, hating himself more than he hated her. He never told her about what he read. He never told another living soul.

Then it was over. His vision let go of its target, his pupils widening as the needle pricked his arm and injected different chemicals. Alan hardly felt a thing, aware of the invasion only by the tug at his flesh. His head motionless, eyes on the same spot, the edges of his vision blurred and darkened. Shadows formed, spreading slowly towards the center, until everything went black. He felt his body relax and his mind let go. Warmth spread through him, which he knew wasn't caused by the concoction running through his veins but by something much more inviting. He let go and the blackness behind the shadows covered him, welcomed him. And he welcomed it.

Shu Len was the first to rise once the weight of their first deceleration lifted. The chemicals in her specially designed mixture insured that. Extra stimulants gave strength to muscles that swung her legs off the couch and her feet onto the deck. She took her medical bag from its secured compartment beneath her chair and ran her eyes over the crew. Those next to her clenched their eyes shut, fighting the urge to cry or shout or ... Shu Len didn't care. It meant they were conscious. The captain struggled to get her legs to respond. Shu Len walked over and laid a hand on her shoulder.

"Don't rush," she said. "Sit for a moment more."

Inessa understood the kindness in Shu Len's voice was order and not request. She lay back as the medic moved on. Shu Len continued to scan the crew, some now moving, groggily unstrapping themselves. She stepped across the room to Alan's chair and stood over him. He lay still, a peaceful look on his face. Shu Len touched him gently, then tapped his cheek.

"Alan, look at me," she said.

His eyes didn't open. She felt his neck, searched for a pulse, and then slapped his face hard.

"Look at me, Alan!" she shouted.

She pounded his chest, felt his neck and bent her ear to his mouth. "Assistance required," she called.

Abede struggled to his feet and stepped over to Alan's chair, previous training making reacting to the medic's two words instinctive and the only thing making his response possible.

"CPR. Start now," Shu Len ordered. She knelt and opened her medical bag, reached in and withdrew an injection pen. Abede immediately began rhythmically pushing on the center of Alan's chest.

"Stand back," she told Abede. He stepped away, panting, and watched as Shu Len tore Alan's gown open. She placed the injector in the gap between two ribs and triggered it. A second passed, then another, and Alan's eyes remained closed.

"Continue CPR," she said, and Abede resumed his place, pumping Alan's chest in an effort to circulate the blood his heart wasn't.

Shu Len withdrew a rectangular box, clicked the side of it and small claws protruded out of the bottom. Abede kept pumping, the droplets of sweat forming on his brow lacking enough gravity to fall.

"Step away," Shu Len ordered.

Abede stepped back until he bumped into the chair behind him. Shu Len forced the box onto Alan's chest and the claws dug in, attaching it to his flesh. She activated the box and moved back. Alan's body convulsed as a jolt of electricity surged through his heart. Shu Len examined the readings coming from the device, and activated it again. Alan's back arched rigidly, and then he lay still. The room was still until his eyes opened wide and he sucked in a mouthful of air with a gasp. Shu Len leaned over as his breathing slowed and became closer to normal.

"Why does my chest hurt?" Alan asked.

"Because I hit it, really hard," Shu Len answered as she pointed a light into his retinas. "Sometimes that is enough to shock the heart back into action. And Abede pressed on it several dozen times, and you have a defibrillator attached to your pectoral muscle."

"That might be it," Alan said. "Why's everybody standing around me?" he asked.

"You flat-lined on release," Shu Len said. She checked his blood pressure, body temperature, and heart readings.

"Can you take this off me?" he asked. "It kind of hurts."

"Not quite yet," Shu Len said. "I need hands. Let's move him to the med couch."

Arms worked their way under Alan, lifted him carefully and moved him to sickbay. Placing him on the medical couch, the crew left he and Shu Len alone. She read the monitor attached to his chest, and then removed the remains of his paper gown. With a pair of scissors, she cut away his sanitary briefs.

"Ah, hey," Alan said. "I can just shower."

"No, you probably couldn't even stand up. Just lie still."

Shu Len removed the sodden diaper, returned with damp cloths and cleaned him. Alan looked around the sickbay as she completed her task. She kept a very orderly and clean workplace, he reflected, trying not to watch the medic cleaning him. Finally, she put the cloths in the recycler and checked his vitals again.

"Sorry about this," Alan said.

"It happens to everybody," she said. "Cross over is tough on the body. My money was on one of the new guys. You cost me a hundred yuan."

"Don't make me laugh. This thing feels like its ripping me open," he said, pointing to the defibrillator attached to his chest.

"That thing is your best friend," Shu Len said. "Now just rest for a few minutes while I wash my own disgusting body. When I come back, we'll run through all the tests and see about clearing you for duty."

Alan started to protest about her body being disgusting until he noticed her stained and wet paper gown. Instead, he simply nodded, closed his eyes, and thought of nothing in particular.

The *Sunspot* decelerated towards the gas giant around which Nyria orbited. After the first deceleration, their view of the planet and its many moons became vividly clear. The large planet glowed pink, its rings reflecting the light from the sun. Many smaller satellites orbited within and near the rings, while several larger moons circled the planet farther out.

"Astrogator Chen," Inessa said. "We have the honor of being the first humans to set eyes on this new world."

Chen smiled at the viewscreen before turning his face to his captain, still beaming. "It is a wonderful system," he reported. "The gas giant is primarily made of hydrogen and nitrogen, like the gas giants at home. The moons are rocky. Two have atmospheres, but one is rather noxious. Heavy on the methane."

"And our target?" Inessa asked.

"Nitrogen, oxygen, traces of argon. Very earthlike. I'm forwarding data to the team as it comes in. Alan was pleased. The first thing he said was that it was breathable. 'Fresh air,' is how he described it."

"Incredible. I look forward to his sampling once we're in orbit," she said.

"Size wise, she's somewhere between earth and Mars," Chen said. "Thanh places the gravity at zero point eight. Do you want him here?"

"No, not yet," Inessa said. "I'll give the team more time to finish their preliminary reports." She stepped across the bridge to where Eva sat at a console.

"Anything?" she asked.

"Background noise," Eva reported. "Nothing directed at us."

"They'd need to be expecting us. And have to have telescopes trained on the sun to see the *Sunspot*," Inessa said. "And a very good telescope at that. What does the background sound like?"

Eva took off her earphone, pressed a button and a faint song like twittering was emitted from the speaker. "Their communication system is sophisticated, in a way," Eva said. "But none of what I'm hearing is of the clarity we received on earth."

"Can we see their transmission? Any images? Television?" Inessa asked.

"They don't seem have to cracked that yet," Eva said. "No evidence of television or digital images, only audio."

"Earth developed radio in the early twentieth century, and television followed a couple decades later. How is it possible there's no pictures?" Inessa asked.

"No idea," Eva answered. "We'll have to ask them if we really want to know. This is all I'm receiving."

"That sound," Inessa said. "It's like—"

"Birds," Eva finished.

"Yes, birds."

"It's a language," Eva said. "The language we received. This is what they sound like. I'm programming the translators now. They should be ready after last decel and we'll be able to listen into the conversation. The information sent in the original message makes it so much easier."

"That's because they wanted to communicate," Inessa said, placing a hand on Eva's shoulder. They listened to the transmissions in silence for a moment.

"We're the first humans to hear this," Inessa said.

Eva reached back and placed her hand on top of Inessa's. "I love this job," she said.

"Keep listening," Inessa said. "We have eighteen hours before next deceleration. Will that be enough for the translator to be ready?"

"It'll be ready," Eva said. "How's Alan?"

"He's fine," Inessa told her. "He slept for twelve hours and woke up as if nothing happened. Shu Len gave him the all clear."

"It's scary when that happens," Eva said. "Send him up if he wants to talk to somebody who's been through the same thing."

"I'll send him if he wants to or not," Inessa said. "What do you think they're saying? Or singing?"

"I ... I don't know. Maybe they're just talking with each other. Or entertaining each other. That's what they'd hear if they listened in on earth," Eva said. "I'll have a clearer idea soon. It's nice just to listen, for now. It feels ... kind of ..."

Inessa closed her eyes and listened with Eva. "Yeah," she agreed. "I know what you mean. It makes me want to just stay and enjoy the sound. But there's prep to finish." She patted the linguist's shoulder and left the bridge.

7

Shu Len monitored each crew member before deceleration. Each test was run just as before, but last decel potentially encouraged a relaxing of vigilance, a feeling that the journey was practically over and they were almost done. But Shu Len knew that most accidents happened close to home and at the tail end of a tiring voyage. She tried not to show Alan the extra attention she paid to his vitals, but it was a charade they both played.

The cold chemicals entered his blood stream as he stared at the ceiling and waited. For the weight, for the memories, for time to drag itself forward, so painfully slowly as the ship finally became stationary. His vision narrowed and he watched the small screen, or rather, what his mind projected onto it. Familiar face. Old stories. And then he saw Shu Len. Watching as she cleaned him with a damp rag, wearing her soiled paper gown, oblivious to her own discomfort or smell.

He watched her face as she worked. He didn't know he was paying that close attention at the time. But there it was, the look in her eyes, the gentle smile on her face. It wasn't just professionalism. It was love.

She loved them all. It was in the way she lifted his arm and wiped it with the cloth. Carefully cleaning the area around the device attached to his chest. Showing no disgust as she cut off the sanitary briefs and cleaned that area, then worked her way down his legs and his feet. His eyes were closed as she did that. How was it possible to watch it now?

The chair shifted and Shu Len's face faded, replaced by Eva. She spoke, her mouth moved, sound left, but fell to the deck, crushed by gravity. She flat lined in the HIP voyage. Shu Len revived her after six minutes of clinical death. Eva talked about the dark over taking her light. Of being terrified on every cross over, and how he would be terrified from now on too. They were part of an exclusive club, one you had to die to enter. He'd find out about the fear on the return voyage, the trip home. He sat in the seat next to her station on the bridge, where Maria sat while she piloted the ship. Eva showed him the planet, magnified on the viewscreen. And then she let him listen. He heard the melodies of their communication as the chair shifted, and mechanical knuckles prodded his flesh. The sound carried him through another rotation, and their final deceleration was complete.

Alan unfastened the straps on his chair and floated off the cushion. The ship ceased rotation on nearing the planet, waiting for Maria to guide it into a discreet orbit. Even the small amount of micro gravity from spin was gone. He pushed off the couch and drifted to the doorway. Shu Len hovered above her charges, smiling at Alan as he passed. He reached out and touched her hand, used his other hand to steady his movement, and floated to the wash station. He removed his gown and pad and used damp towels to clean himself. Stuffing the used towels into the recycler, he used hand rails to pull himself to his quarters where he put on his dress uniform. Despite her feelings about the military, Inessa wanted the team to look professional. Alan knew that dressing the same in a ship orbiting above a planet whose inhabitants never knew they were there didn't add competence or skill in any way. But his captain saw purpose in it so he dressed as ordered.

He fumbled with buttons, caught his belt as it tried to drift away, started to spin slowly as he put on socks. It was all ceremonial. They would look the part of voyaging astronauts and taikonauts and cosmonauts, even if nobody but themselves ever saw. He straightened his body before the mirror and examined himself. Sky blue, collared shirt, green straight legged trousers, soft-soled white shoes. White neck tie. Green, blue and white—the colors of earth. He drifted out of his quarters and joined a growing group on the bridge. Alan smiled as he entered, and saw smiles on the others. They watched the planet below, whisps of white cloud passing over a dark blue ocean that framed a large continent. Beyond the planet, the massive gas giant filled the screen, sunlight reflected in the rings radiating from its equator.

"Well done, team," Inessa said

Alan patted Dave on the shoulder, which sent him floating away. He didn't go far in the control room designed for four.

"Maria has established a high planetary orbit for you to work from," Inessa said. "But first, let's just enjoy the view, and then retire to the mess. I have a surprise waiting."

Sachets of champagne, caviar in tubes, crackers and cheese that the captain always packed to celebrate arrival. The first job after the party was always vacuuming crumbs from the air. But for the moment, the crew floated in silence, staring at the image on the viewscreen.

The comms line crackled and everybody flinched. A twitter like bird song filled the bridge.

"Eva?" Inessa asked.

"That's a different frequency from the chatter below," she said. "Stronger. Clearer."

"Is the translator functioning?"

"It is," Eva said.

The comms emitted more bird song. All eyes turned from the screen to Eva. She swiped her screen and touched an icon. The bird song ceased, replaced by the human voice programmed into the translator.

"Welcome to Nyria," the voice said. "We are so happy you have answered our call, and that you have come. Welcome. Welcome. Welcome.

"We are so happy you have come. Please reply on this frequency." The translator conveyed the excitement in the speaker's voice. "We welcome you to Nyria. Please reply."

"Who are they talking to?" Maria asked.

"It sounds like us," Jardin answered.

"That isn't possible," Inessa said. "How can they know we are here? Eva, do you detect any sensors? Anything targeting the ship?"

"Just the message," Eva answered. "It's a tight beam straight to us."

The crew turned from Eva to Inessa, then back to the linguist.

"We welcome you to Nyria," the planet said again. "We are sending this message in a different format."

The comms went silent and digits flashed across Eva's screen. After several seconds it stopped.

"Well?" Inessa asked.

"It's the code of the original messages," Eva answered. "The message received on earth."

"That's not exactly what I wanted to know."

"It's a welcome," Eva reported.

"Read it," Inessa said.

"We welcome to the planet Nyria our visitors from afar. We are so happy that you have answered our call, and that you have come so far to meet us. We await your response." Eva turned in her chair after she finished reading. "That's all it says before repeating. Do I respond?" she asked.

"No, you don't respond," Inessa said. "We don't respond. We aren't here for a first contact. We study and we return. That is our mission."

"Is this normal?" Dave asked Alan. "Has this ever happened?"

"No," Alan answered. "This isn't normal. It doesn't happen. It's never happened before."

"Be quiet," Inessa said. "Please," she offered to soften the order.

"It looks like the game is up, Captain," Gunther said. "First contact has been made."

"Please," Inessa repeated. "Quiet." She drifted closer to Eva, took hold of the linguist's chair and leaned into the screen. Digits continued to flow across, repeating the message of welcome.

"There's lots of traffic on the other channels," Eva said. "I think the cat's out of the bag."

"Meaning?"

"They're talking about us," Eva said, pointing to the bud in her ear. "The whole planet. Alien visitors, space ship, that kind of thing. Do you want to listen?"

"Not just yet," Inessa said.

"Lots of excitement down there," Eva continued. "There's also lots of fear, on some channels. They don't know who we are, or why we are here. You can imagine. Aliens showing up—"

"Eva, please," Inessa said.

"We have to answer," Jardin said.

"I know that," Inessa said. She stared at the screen as the others waited. She finally pushed away and drifted to the middle of the bridge.

"There is no precedent for this," she said to the crew. "But there is a protocol. It is very clear. We are to leave orbit, leave the system, and return to earth."

She didn't have to wait long for a protest. As the captain, all responsibility sat on her shoulders, but she wanted to hear what her crew thought.

"We've come too far," Alan said. "And I sure as hell don't want rush back."

"We can move farther away, to the other large moon," Maria suggested. "Or within the rings."

"They know we are here," Ariana said. "Hiding isn't going to change that."

"Neither is going home," Gunther said. "They have made contact. First contact. We have responded and we are here. Protocol makes no sense in this situation."

"If we respond, we may never be sent out again," Inessa said. "This will be our last trip. All of us," Inessa said. "You will never fly again."

"You don't know that," Eva said. "There is no precedent. You said that. How we react is what is important—"

"And they have initiated contact," Gunther added. "What we do next will establish future protocol."

"To return without responding would be worse than never flying again. I would carry the shame and the regret for the rest of my life." They all turned towards Thanh. He shook his head. "To be at the door, to be invited in, and to turn away…" He indicated to the planet on the viewscreen. "If we do that, I would never fly again anyway."

"Our actions might affect the *Concurrent* mission," Abede said.

Gunther shook his head. "That's three hundred years from now."

"But it is a point we have to consider," Inessa said. "We have no doubt already become part of this civilization's history."

"Then we have already impacted *Concurrent*," Gunther said.

"Our presence is already contact. First contact has been made. There is no logical reason not to respond. It is *fait acompli*."

Jardin's words had a finality that ended the discussion. Nobody spoke to counter, or to support. They gazed in silence at the image on the viewscreen. The shadow of the planet made a small dark spot on the gas giant behind it. The blue of its oceans looked like a cloak wrapped around the green land.

"Play the message again," Inessa told Eva. "Without translator."

Eva activated the comms and birdsong filled the bridge. Inessa raised a hand to her mouth. She felt a hand on her shoulder and knew it was Gunther's. Alan felt a hand take his and glanced down to see Maria holding it. He placed his other hand gently on Dave's shoulder, careful not to upset the other man's balance.

"Okay, Eva," Inessa said. "That's enough. Please turn it down. I believe we have consensus. Am I correct?"

Nods and murmurs of ascent followed.

"Eva, prepare to send a message. Utilize the translator so they know we can understand them. They will hear us in their own language. Be brief. We need time to think through what we are doing," Inessa said. "I want us to reconvene in the mess where we can at least have something to eat. And drink."

"What do I say?" Eva asked.

"Say ... No, tell them: 'Message to follow'."

8

The platter sat on the messroom table, attached to the surface to prevent it from floating. Tubes of caviar and packets of crackers adorned it, each similarly attached. Most of the sachets of champagne floated empty near the ceiling. Inessa squeezed some of the fish eggs onto a cracker and took a bite. Small crumbs drifted away from her mouth. It wasn't the most practical of foods in freefall, but it was how special events were marked in her family in Volgograd, as well as her other family on the *Sunspot*.

Typically, the crew joined her at the table as a relaxing reward at the end of a taxing journey. The following weeks of research and data collection typically waited for the morrow. This celebration was far from relaxing or typical. Few looked rested. She doubted any took advantage of the short rest period to catch up on sleep. Excitement crackled through the compartment. The treats on the table served only to momentarily pause conversations.

Inessa finished her cracker and tapped the table with her knuckles. "Eva has been monitoring communications on the planet," she said.

"I think we should hear from her before we proceed." She lifted her hand towards the linguist.

"I think our message made it worse." Eva said. "It got their attention, though."

Eva sipped from her drink sachet. "There's too much traffic to monitor it all, but we're the topic of conversation on practically every channel."

"As you can imagine," Inessa said.

"There's a great deal of excitement. Just like there would be at home," Eva continued. "But also, a lot of fear."

"Just like there would be at home," Alan agreed. "Fear in terms of an unknown," Eva said. "As if in what kind of threat we may pose. Our technology is obviously far superior to theirs. Simply by being here they are aware of that."

"And nothing more from the senders? No tight beam?" Inessa asked.

"No. They seem to be waiting for that message," Eva said. "I'd like Gunther to deploy a comms drone so I can get a better idea of what's happening."

"We shouldn't do anything that might appear aggressive," Chen said. "Launching probes could be seen as an attack."

"Agreed," Inessa said.

"I think we need to contact them soon," Eva added. "The sooner the better. They … deserve that much."

"Agreed. We will respond shortly. Let them know who we are, where we are from, and what our intentions are. We'll keep it simple until we know more about them. Communication will only be with the senders of the message. What they do with it, who they share it with, is their affair. Science team, prepare your probes, but do not initiate research until we can tell them what we're doing. Nothing we do can be perceived as a potentially hostile act."

"But prepare to collect data as planned?" Thanh asked.

"Yes," Inessa answered. "It just might have to be negotiated this time. Collect data in unpopulated areas, and any technology sent to the surface must be programmed to self-destruct in the case of any malfunction. Protocols remain the same."

"Except for the biggest protocol," Jardin said. Some of them laughed.

"Except for the biggest," Inessa agreed. "I would have liked this moment to be a celebration, as a way to say well done, to all of you, before we start the next phase of our journey. But everything is different. As always, I am very proud of you. Thank you." She raised from her seat and gripped the table to stay in place. "Eva and I are going to contact our friends down below now."

The room was silent. Inessa and Eva pushed off the table and drifted away from the table. At the bridge, Inessa took Eva's seat, and the linguist prepared the comms for her.

"Okay, just press that part of the screen and talk," Eva instructed. "They'll hear what you say, but in their own language."

"No second takes?"

"No, ma'am, you're going live," Eva said. "You can speak Russian if you are more comfortable."

"No, English is fine," Inessa said. "I rehearsed it in English, at least in my head. Let's not keep them waiting. Make it ship wide so the crew can hear."

Eva hung in the air silently as Inessa reached a finger towards the screen. She took a deep breath and pressed the screen.

"To the peoples of Nyria: greetings from the crew of the interstellar starship, *Sunspot,* and from all of humanity on the planet Earth.

You have reached across the stars, offering an outstretched hand as a peaceful greeting. We respond to your invitation, offering our hand in return. We come in peace and friendship. Your message has travelled three hundred light years and found our planet, located in the spiral arm of our shared galaxy. Our home, Earth, is a planet of many peoples, from many lands and cultures. But we have come together for this mission of good will. We, the crew of the *Sunspot,* are ambassadors for the human race, and are privileged to be the hand of our people."

Inessa lifted her hands to signal the end of her message and Eva touched the viewscreen.

"And sent," she said. "Well done, Captain."

"My god, that was nerve wracking," Inessa said.

"'The hand of our people' ... nice touch."

"Thanks. I stole it from Moreno. From his speech to the crews on earth."

"I thought you didn't like to improvise," Eva said.

"I don't. But things change."

"There's a message coming in," Eva said.

"As expected," Inessa said. "Play it."

Eva reached over her captain again and activated the message.

"Crew of the *Sunspot*," the translator said. "We, the peoples of Nyria, are humbled and honored by your efforts to cross such a vast distance to reach us. We acknowledge the magnitude of this moment. We feel with deep emotion, this meeting of two species. We look forward to continuing contact, of learning and sharing, and invite you to our home."

"End of message," Eva said. "That sounds like they're asking us to land."

"They are," Inessa said. "Send a message asking them for a private line with the director of the messaging project, if they have such a person. Can you do that?"

"I can request that," Eva said. "You expected this?"

"I expected something like it," Inessa answered. "Improvisation doesn't mean you can't have a plan. Landing might endanger both them and us. So, I tell them that we need to conduct research before we are certain it is safe, that we exchange good will and not disease. We have enough experience on earth of cultures being wiped out by introduced illnesses. I think they will agree to our probes collecting data."

"That sounds like they have a choice."

"It's polite to give them that impression," Inessa said. "Gunther," she said through ship wide comms, "stand by to launch science probes as soon as I get an affirmative response from the planet."

Alan sat next Gunther, each studying the screen in front of them. Gunther looked through the probe's eyes as it entered the planet's upper atmosphere. Heat flared red as it descended, fading away as it leveled out at one hundred kilometers, and travelled in the winds of the upper atmosphere. Alan studied the readings on his monitor, measured the air, its chemical make-up, the level of particulates. He indicated for Gunther to take the probe lower, into the strong winds circulating far above the surface. Wings extended and locked into place, it caught the current and effortlessly glided in at high speed. Gunther adjusted the monitor until it faced Alan. Alan's eyes went from the stream of data on his monitor to the image of high cloud. He liked this part.

"Handing over control," Gunther said

"I got her," Alan confirmed.

Gunther floated away from station. "Take care of my girl. Auto-return is programmed, you know the—"

"I know it," Alan said, smiling. "Go help Thanh collect some rocks, I've got work to do."

Alan returned to the monitors and didn't see Gunther leave the room. He adjusted the view of the probe's camera and the planet's surface spread below. Blue ocean passed for miles as the winds took the probe south to the equator, before meeting the super continent. Alan guided the probe lower, turned to the other monitor and read the data streaming in. A substantial urban center lay to the east but elements that dominated earth's atmosphere at a similar period of technological development were either absent or only in trace amounts. Sulfur dioxide was present, evidence of geothermal activity and clear indications of its use as a source of power. Nowhere did he see levels indicating the burning of fossil fuels for transportation or industry.

Carbon dioxide surface concentrations were healthy, especially in the dense arboreal regions of the north, but consistent around the planet. Accumulations of nitrogen dioxide were rare. Data indicated pockets of carbon monoxide, of levels that indicated only volcanic or thermal origin. Particulate matter measured normal, natural dusts blown through the atmosphere.

Alan initiated the dispersal sequence and doors on the belly of the probe opened. He checked each micro-probe before sending it out, and soon a dozen smaller probes were scooting through the air, each collecting specialized data. He tracked them for several minutes, colored lights on a monitor, to ensure they followed their pre-programmed courses. Satisfied, he returned his attention to the primary probe, watching the planet below. Adjusting course, Alan directed the probe towards a range of mountains, following the windward side.

The probe passed through cloud and the chemical composition of the precipitation scrolled across Alan's monitor. He flew lower, capturing air samples brought over by seasonal winds and trapped along the ridge, including particulates carried from the cities to collect in the foothills. The probe followed the line marking where a long fertile valley met rocky hills and mountains. Alan scanned for the large disc and radio tower the original transmission was sent from, deliberately taking the probe over the vicinity to be seen by those below. An airship flew to the north and he directed the probe towards it, coming within four hundred meters before swerving away and continuing on the pre-planned course. He didn't doubt most of the planet were following the progress of his research, even sending up airships to investigate closer. Alan hoped none of the slow-moving vehicles got in the way.

He directed the probe higher, over the summit and followed the drier, leeward side of the range. The vegetation below turned from greens to browns and yellows, and the terrain flattened and spread in a sprawling savannah. Kilometer after kilometer passed below until Alan followed a great river that dissected the plain. Abede intended to send a sampling pod into its waters to sample biological content. Alan guided the probe along its course as it wound its way to the distant ocean before he increased altitude and returned the probe to the pre-programmed course circling the moon and focused on mapping weather patterns, wind strengths, and the atmosphere. He scanned the data feed, breathing in deeply, as if tasting the air outside the probe through the numbers it returned.

Checking the time, he made his way to his appointment at communications. *We would like to meet you and your crew. Can you each speak with a designated liaison at the station? And send a message to the people of Nyria?* the station's Director asked. Inessa agreed. A widely broadcast statement, introducing themselves to the people of Nyria, then informal *conversations* with members of their team, conducted one to one on a special frequency. The translator offered several potential meanings to the word, conversations, sensing deeper meaning in the pitch or tone used in the asking. To converse, to commune, to form union ... Inessa saw it as a way to develop a relationship and give her team the time they needed to collect the data they sought.

Alan sat in Eva's chair and let her set up the session. She helped nestle the translator bud into his ear, showed him how to mute the broadcast should the need arise, and how to initiate a one-to-one link with the operator, his liaison, on the surface. As Eva pushed off the chair and drifted out of the bridge, Alan cleared his throat, took a sip from a drink tube and let his finger hover over the screen. He breathed out quickly and activated the link.

"Hello," he began. "My name is Alan Edward Reading and I am the atmospheric scientist on board the interstellar vessel, *Sunspot*."

"Welcome, Alan Edward Reading, of the earth ship, *Sunspot*," he was answered. "We have many listeners who are very interested in meeting you."

"Thank you," Alan said, trying hard not to think about who he was talking to, or how many were listening. He imagined another school group, or community organization on earth, one of the dozens on routine speaking tours after each mission. It didn't work. He was still nervous.

"We are ready to *receive* you," the voice from below said, the translator again offering multiple meanings.

"I have never spoken to an entire planet before, so please excuse me if I am slow to start," Alan said. "It is an honor to address you." He had the speech memorized, and repeated different variations on many occasions. But those words failed him, seeming not only inappropriate, but disingenuous. "What is the way, in your culture, to start such a meeting?" Alan found himself asking.

"I have never spoken to visitors from another world," the voice answered. "But you are kind in your query. Let us start as we would in my place of birth. I gaze into your eyes and breathe deeply. I invite you to know that I am open and receptive to knowing you. That I see you. Then I close my eyes and bow my head slightly, to indicate I am ready to receive, and I meet your eyes again."

"Thank you," Alan said. They have eyes and heads, he thought, however the translator interprets it. "I gaze into your eyes and breathe deeply," Alan paused and inhaled, exhaling slowly. "I invite you to know that I am receptive to knowing you. I close my eyes and bow my head, and I meet your eyes again."

"Thank you, Alan Edward Reading. That is a beautiful image," the voice said.

"What is your name?" Alan asked.

"My name?" He heard a sound that may have been a giggle, but sounded more like chirp. "I did not expect that question. My name is Ceera. I am a technician here at the Stellar Messaging Project. There are many people listening who want to know about you. Can you tell them about your home world?"

"Yes, of course," Alan replied. "I have seen a great river, crossing the savannah and making its way to the sea. I was born near a river, but not one so grand. My river flows from a mountain range that forms the spine of my state. Cold waters join together to form what is known as the Sacramento River, which flows through the capital city, also called Sacramento. The name is from another language, which translates to a special, or sacred, act."

Alan paused, suddenly at a loss as to how to continue. He reached for the mute button to collect his thoughts. Before he could press, Ceera cut in.

"Such a lovely name," she observed. "Do your mountains have names?"

"Names, yes," Alan said. "Everything has a name. The mountains are called the Sierra Nevadas. They stand in the east. Sacramento sits in a long and fertile valley, framed by the Sierras in the east, and the coastal range in the west. It is a beautiful place. The Sacramento River flows out of this valley and into a great bay where a wonderful city sits. That city is called San Francisco, named after a saintly man. It is always a joy to visit. So, I grew up between the sea and the mountains. Summers were always very warm and we often vacationed in both."

"And the *we* you speak of, Alan. Who are *we*?"

"Oh. My family," Alan answered. "My parents, and my brother and sister, would pile into a hover-pod and spend time in nature. A vacation."

"Some words seem to translate slowly, Alan," Ceera said. "You are speaking of a unit bound by shared genetics? Can you say more about this unit?"

Stay away from any discussion involving advanced technology, military capability, and economic systems. Keep to safe and neutral subjects. Do not feed our hosts information about us while we are ignorant of them, Inessa told them. That wasn't quite accurate, Alan thought, they already knew more about those on the planet. Their original transmission gave a great deal of information. Carbon based, bi-pedal, mammalian. But the information sent did lack certain specifics. It was safe and neutral. Alan felt he was on a safe subject. Although some families are neither safe nor neutral, he was grateful that his was.

"A unit ... yes, a family is a unit bound by genetics," Alan said, the audience hearing human laughter for the first time. "My dad grew up in the mountains, so he loved returning, taking us into the wilderness and camping. My mother lived in San Francisco until she was a teenager, so she shared her love of that place. Both my brother and sister are older than me, but there wasn't much of an age difference between us, so we did a lot of things together."

"Please, tell us more. What is this group of people?"

"A family is ... I have been away so much that I haven't had a lot of time to think about that," Alan responded, "but it is a bond, a connection, that exits in time, the time you are all together, as you all grow and mature and age. I can recall so many memories, so many moments, that shaped who I am. All the shared experiences, the shared past. But it also exists outside of time, even outside of space or place. As I think of them now they are with me, in a way. Some moments are very simple and special. Like when I was a very young boy out in the garden with my brother and father, and he taught us how to squat down close to the ground and not get our knees or bottoms wet. It must have recently rained. But I felt like such a big boy at that moment, like I was being given a secret of the grown-up world. You see? As I remember, I am once again six years old, and he a young father with the world at his feet."

He continued speaking to the screen and those below followed his stories of swimming in mountain lakes, of snowball fights at his grandmother's house, camp fires by the river with beer and friends as a teenager, memories that took him back to a simpler time. Before he realized how much time had slipped by, Ceera interrupted his reflections.

"Alan Edward Reading, I am sorry, but our allotted broadcast time is coming to a close," she said. "Thank you for such a personal glimpse into your life. For such a special gift, we are very grateful. Although I am sure many, like myself, have so many questions to ask! We look forward to hearing so much more."

"That would be nice," Alan said.

Silence followed. Alan looked over his shoulder for Eva but she had left him to his interview and the bridge was empty except for the pilot. He moved his finger to the screen to sever the link when Ceera spoke again.

"Thank you, Alan Edward Reading. Your talk was very special. Very personal." There was a pause before she continued. "You are no longer speaking to the whole of Nyria. It is only me."

"I am sorry it was not more planned," he said, relaxing.

"You were wonderful! We just want to hear about you," Ceera said. "To hear from Alan Edward Reading."

"I was nervous before we began. And just Alan. Call me Alan."

"One name," Ceera said. "Same-same. We have a commonality! I look forward to hearing more about you, Alan."

"And I know nothing of you," he answered. "Where did you grow up? Who are your family? Do you have any siblings?"

"Now I am not prepared," Ceera said. "I did not expect questions."

A moment passed and Alan thought the conversation was at an end as soon as it began.

"My formative years were in the city south of this location," Ceera said. "Your memories brought up some of my own, not as pleasant. But I also recalled a small lake held in rocky hands, high where the air is crisp and cold. There is a cabin there, warm and inviting, not far from here. It has always been a special place to me, a place I haven't visited in far too long. Thank you for helping the image resurface. I will hold it and reflect."

"It sounds nice," Alan said. "Was it with your parents?"

"With others. My colleagues at the station. Not the type of genetically linked unit you have described."

"Family."

"Yes, that was the word you used," Ceera said. "It is a word that seems to describe my colleagues. I would very much like to speak with you again, to explore what it means to be human. What it means to be Alan."

"That sounds too one sided," Alan said. "I know very little of you. Except for your name. And a small cabin in the mountains."

"I am sure you will learn more," Ceera said. "I can send times when we may have access to communications."

"That would be nice," he answered.

"Until then. I will sign off now. It has been a privilege and a pleasure, Alan."

"It has indeed, Ceera," he said, putting a finger to the screen and ending the connection.

"Did you just make a date with an alien?" Maria asked.

Alan turned, taking notice of the pilot for the first time since beginning his broadcast. "I think I might have," he said.

9

Alan reviewed the mass of data acquired by the probe as it circled the planet. He joined Gunther at the docking bay as it returned to the *Sunspot*. The craft entered the ship and parked itself in a secured bay, sealed with the other surface probes and their samples. Despite their findings, all samples would remain closed off from human contact until their return, and only then accessed in a secure laboratory at Luna Base. Wise precaution, but useless in this case. All the data read benevolent. The air was not only breathable, it was also very clean.

It was, Alan wrote in his preliminary report to Inessa, healthier for them to inhale than the recycled stuff they were all breathing on the ship, and even what they breathe at home. Abede joined Alan and Thanh at the table in the ready room. Abede complained, as he did each voyage: that his data was cursory, that he needed more time, that a planet deserved longer. Thanh's samples contained vials of alien bacteria, archaea and other prokaryotes, single celled life forms with simple DNA structures, as well as tissue samples from unsuspecting, more complex life forms, collected by insect sized probes. Each needle from the small fliers providing a biopsy, analyzed as soon as it arrived back on the waiting probe. Both their findings aligned with Alan's.

"Where is Inessa?" Thanh asked.

"Still on comms," Abede said. "Speaking with the Director."

"Your broadcast was genius," Alan said. "What was that you played?"

"It was a *kora*. A traditional lute, from home. Although the songs were more contemporary. I borrowed from a very famous performer," Abede answered. "Yours was enjoyable. Very hometown, if that's the right word."

"Hometown?" Alan laughed. "That's a word, anyway. I couldn't remember anything I prepared and just vomited into the mic."

"No," Thanh disagreed, "it was nice. Very genuine."

"Thanks."

"You seem to be on the comms quite regularly," Abede said. "What is her name?"

"Ceera."

"Do you talk about your home town?" Thanh asked.

"And hers," Alan answered. "Though last time I read poetry."

The two men laughed. "Where I come from," Abede said, "that is called courtship."

Gunther left the comms station, gave a small push and drifted out of the bridge, hardly noticing Alan as he passed him in the corridor. At the junction to crew quarters, he turned in the air, tapped the wall and disappeared around the corner. Alan entered the bridge and took the seat just vacated. Maria sat her station, maintaining watch, which consisted of watching the planet below and trying to tune out the incessant conversations from the comms station. Once the orbit was programmed, there was little else for the pilot to do except keep an eye on the controls.

"Lonely watch. Where's Eva?" he asked.

"Staying away from her station," Maria said. "Somebody always seems to be taking her seat. She's probably working in her quarters."

Alan shrugged and started pulling up the link to the surface.

"Anything wrong?" Maria asked.

"No, just making conversation."

"Well, you'd better make your call. Times wasting. Don't spend it talking to me."

Alan listened for sarcasm or resentment in her voice but didn't find any. He swiped the screen and tapped an icon. He heard a twitter and listened, smiling. It repeated, with a slight change in tone. He activated the translator.

"Alan, are you there?" Ceera asked.

"I'm here, Ceera," he answered. "It is such a pleasure to hear you again."

"As it is to hear you," Ceera answered.

"I need a raise," Maria muttered. She inserted noise cancelling buds in her ears and reviewed orbital data.

Alan watched Maria turn towards her screen before returning to his. It was easy to forget she was there, but remembering brought self-consciousness. He pushed that feeling aside and spoke to Ceera.

"I've been thinking about what you asked, about being human," he said after a moment. "That's not an easy question to answer. I think there are too many answers already."

"You cannot get out of it that easily, Alan," Ceera said.

"I know," he answered, "you told me of the goddess and her rings, always in your sky, how some devote their lives to her, never really questioning who they are. That sounds familiar. It's very human. I mean, the same thing happens on earth. People looking to a god or goddess, devoting their lives to what they might represent. But I think of it as metaphor. When you say that word, *goddess*, the translator has a little difficulty. I look forward to understanding what it means to you."

"Of course."

"But they all imply something bigger, that we are part of something bigger. Somehow linked to a wholeness," Alan said. "It something most humans continually seek."

"*Union*," Ceera said.

"Yes," Alan said. "That's another word the translator seems to stutter over."

"Do they seek union with all other humans, to no longer be an individual, but a member of a collective?" she asked

"No, not like that," Alan answered. "Not at all. We are always solitary individuals, but ... I don't know. We feel like we lack wholeness, until we find it in something bigger. Or in life itself. Or in another."

Silence sat between them as Ceera waited and Alan grasped for ways to go on. "There was a poet over two centuries ago that touched this union and tried to describe his experience. He found union in not only another, but in everything. He ... he couldn't find distinction between himself and the universe, and yet found it affirm his sense of self."

"He sounds like a holy man," Ceera said.

"He wasn't. He was just a poet," Alan said. "But maybe he was. Yes, I think he was, but never seen as such. He wrote a very long poem, with lots of verse, bound into a book, and then he spent the rest of his life revising it. I think the first edition was the rawest, the closest to his experience. In it he describes humanity, in all its glory, good and bad. Though he judges nothing as good or bad. All was beautiful and wonderful."

"Why are you making me wait, Alan?" Ceera asked. "You have this book, don't you?"

"Yes, I do. I brought a copy as part of my weight allowance."

"Alan!"

"Okay," he said. "But it is too long to read all at once. I'll only give you a taste."

"Read to me, Alan," Ceera said.

"This part is named, *Song of Myself*," Alan said, "Though in the first edition, he did not title the sections."

Alan felt Ceera's impatience and eagerness, and began to read:

"*I celebrate myself, and sing myself, and what I assume, you shall assume, for every atom belonging to me as good belongs to you.*

"*I loafe and invite my soul, I lean and loafe at my ease observing a spear of summer grass ...*

"*Houses and rooms are full of perfumes, the shelves are crowded with perfumes, I breathe the fragrance myself and know it and like it, the distillation would intoxicate me also, but I shall not let it.*

"*The atmosphere is not a perfume, it has no taste of the distillation, it is odorless, it is for my mouth forever, I am in love with it, I will go to the bank by the wood and become undisguised and naked, I am mad for it to be in contact with me ...*

"*There never was any more inception than there is now, nor any more youth or age than there is now, and will never be any more perfection than there is now, nor any more heaven or hell than there is now.*"

Alan stopped reading and listened. A faint, untranslatable sound filtered through. He wondered what it sounded like when Nyrians cried. Conscious of a presence behind him, he glanced back to see Jardin waiting for his session at comms. Alan ignored him and turned to the screen.

"Are you there?" he asked.

"Yes, I am here," Ceera answered.

"I will need to read more at another time," he said.

"I would like that," Ceera replied. "This poet. He sounds like he is a Nyrian."

"He would probably say he was," Alan said.

"*There will never be any more perfection than there is now ...*" she repeated. "I look forward to hearing more, Alan."

He signed off. Jardin took the seat as soon he vacated it. "You realize, my friend," he said. "That reading poetry to a woman in most cultures is referred to as courting."

"Somebody recently told me that," Alan answered, drifting out of the room.

Inessa floated into the room wearing a smile. It faded when she saw the three scientists at the table and she remembered why they were there. Their planned research, their mission brief, was complete. The data requested from the ISA was acquired and their mission was scheduled to enter its next phase, return. She noticed a change in their own expressions as she grabbed the back of her chair and pulled herself into it. As if they remembered too.

"Thank you for your reports, and your very thorough and professional work," she said.

They looked back at her, silent.

"Gunther has let me know that the probes and samples are secured for the teams on Luna. Time for a well-earned rest," she added.

"There is so much more to do," Thanh said. "Rest is the last thing I want."

"I understand—"

"It is a wonderful biosphere, perfectly benign, perfectly fascinating," Thanh said. "I have studied my whole life, prepared my whole life, for such an opportunity to explore, to learn—"

"I understand."

"Then why secure all the samples and stop work?" Thanh asked.

"Protocol," Abede said. "It is what we do with exotic specimens. Even if they are harmless. They are harmless, by the way," he added to Inessa. "You know that."

"I know."

"And after our scheduled data collection is complete, it is secured for return," Abede continued. "It is what we do, even when we don't have to."

"So why talk about returning?" Alan asked. "We don't have to rush home. We control time. We can stay a year and return a day after we left."

"We do not control time," Inessa replied firmly. "And that is one protocol I will not break. Time spent here is time spent away from earth. That is not negotiable."

Alan waited a respectful moment before continuing. He spoke quietly. "Okay," he said. "Elapse protocol is untouchable. Time passing is time passing. That's not the protocol I want to talk about."

"It is not for us to discuss this," Abede said. "The whole crew must be here."

"What are we doing?" Thanh asked.

"Talking about your research. About the planet being benign. About us being benign," Alan answered. "You want to stay longer," he said to Inessa.

"It is not about my wants," Inessa said.

"Why not? Make a decision, issue an order," Alan said. "You're the captain."

"This is too big a decision for even a captain to make," Inessa said. "I do not want my own emotional feelings to jeopardize the careers of everybody on the ship."

"Haven't we already passed that point?" Alan said. "I mean, about what we do next, not your emotions. I don't think anything we do from here will make a difference about our careers. Way too late for that."

"That's not true," Inessa said. "We have been confronted with a changed situation and we responded effectively."

"Same-same," Alan replied.

"What?" Inessa asked.

"A changed situation," Alan said. "The planet being safe, and our presence expected. We responded the way we did, and nothing can take that back. The ISA may never trust us again. So, what we do next doesn't matter regarding that."

"Call the crew," Abede suggested.

"I mean, it's a discussion we already had," Alan persisted.

"No, we haven't. Speaking with the Nyrians is one thing, landing is completely different," Inessa said.

"We are going to land?" Thanh asked.

"Then let's call the crew together. What are we waiting for?" Abede persisted.

"I called you here to thank you for your work, not argue with you," Inessa said.

"Shall I call the crew then?" Abede asked.

Inessa gritted her teeth and pursed her lips, staring at the table before turning to Abede and nodding. He pushed off his chair and floated to a wall, taking a handhold with one hand and activating shipwide comms with the other. "All crew to the messroom," he said, before letting go of the wall and gliding out of the ready room.

The others followed. Inessa took her time, entering the mess after everybody had arrived and taken their seats at the table. She reached her place and pulled her body into the seat, attaching the Velcro strap held her in place. Her crew waited in silence for her to finish. She looked around the table and made eye contact with each one. She smiled.

"Thank you for coming," she started. "The science team have completed their scheduled research. The probes and samples are secured in the lazaret. Their preliminary findings show that the atmosphere, and the biosphere, is benign, and that we pose no threat to life on the planet."

"What's a lazaret?" Dave interrupted.

"The quarantine chamber," she answered as if flicking away a pesky mosquito.

"This mission is not like any other," she continued. "We have made first contact. You have all spoken to an entire planet, and I believe have even cultivated friendships with those below." She waited for questions but none came. A few nodded but no one offered an opinion, yet.

"I myself have spoken many times with the Director of the messaging project. He is aware that our research is complete, and protocol mandates our return to earth. But he has extended an invitation. He has asked if the crew of the *Sunspot* would honor their team, and their planet, by visiting them on the surface."

She lifted a hand to preempt any interruption.

"I would like to accept their invitation," she said. "I want to go to the surface. I want to meet the Director. And I want you to come with me. I do not want to turn my back and go home without ... I feel a connection I cannot explain. But this cannot be about my emotions. I want to make clear, of my feelings, and this: You know what I would like do, but I am open to be dissuaded. If you disagree with this course of action, let me hear your reasoning."

She tried to sit back in zero gravity, and pushed against the table to make it happen. She kept her hands on the surface of the table, one on top of the other, and waited. They all waited, but nobody spoke.

"Okay," Inessa finally said. "I am very happy. Ariana, help Gunther prepare the shuttle for an atmospheric descent and landing."

"I'll help too," Maria said. "I need to create a flight plan."

"Of course," Inessa agreed. "And Eva, can you prepare translator devices so our hosts can understand us on the ground?"

"I already started," Eva answered. "Noor has given me specification for their ears."

"Noor?" Inessa asked.

"My ... *liaison* on the surface," Eva replied.

Inessa smiled at the choice of description, and noticed others doing the same.

"Shall I prep a printer for descent?" Eva asked. "It's sophisticated technology, but we're going to need more devices on the surface."

"We're bringing a flier to the surface, there's not much more sophisticated than that," Maria said.

Inessa nodded to Eva. "Yes, a printer will be needed." She looked at the crew, who appeared to be waiting for more.

"Well, let's get ready," she said as a dismissal.

"Wait," Chen asked. "Who will stay behind with the ship?"

"No way," Alan said. "That's too much to ask anybody. Stay behind?"

"Nobody will be staying behind," Inessa clarified. "The *Sunspot* will function on autopilot until we return from the planet. We will monitor her from the surface according to a watch schedule, just as if we were aboard."

"I'd ask about protocol, but I think I know what the answer will be," Dave said.

"The only protocol that remains paramount is that the technology of folding does not fall into extra-terrestrial hands. Primary Protocol remains. The self-destruct sequence will initiate if that were ever to happen. But that is extremely unlikely as the Nyrians do not possess the ability to reach orbit."

10

The gas giant disappeared from view as the shuttle nosed down and began its descent. The cold calm of space was replaced with frantic waves of color. A glow danced outside the windows as the shielding shed the heat generated through the thickening air meeting the skin of the shuttle. The ship rocked violently as it sliced through the atmospheric layers. Stars vanished and darkness lifted as the pink and blue sky of Nyria shown through the shuttle windows.

Maria guided the craft into the lower atmosphere, extended the wings and brought the nose up. She heard a shared groan behind her as the crew were pushed back into their chairs. Her own stomach threatened to revolt, but Shu Len's medicine stopped them from throwing up. Alan rubbed his legs as they felt pressure after weeks of orbiting in weightlessness. Although the planet below was seventy-five percent of the gravity of earth, there was no doubt that their first steps would be difficult and their feet unsteady.

Their target in the continent below grew larger as they descended. The grey of the huge radio disc stood out from the surrounding green. The shuttle arced gradually and the crew stared at the scene. A small settlement was the only permanent companion of the disc. It was built to house the technicians operating the station and no other town or city lay nearby. As the shuttle sank further, a small group of long, cylindrical airships came into view, tethered to their mooring poles. The Director explained to Inessa that the world wanted a live description of the historic encounter, and would she mind if the media attended? They would be confined to their area and not interfere with the meeting, he assured her. It was common practice for the crew of the *Sunspot* to speak in front of microphone or camera, as well as tour to speak and share their experiences visiting distant worlds, so of course, she gave no objection.

The shuttle buffeted as it hit low atmospheric turbulence, but Maria quickly brought it through to calmer air. No one spoke as details on the surface became clearer. A forest canopy, grassy clearings, a thin road winding over hills and into a nearby mountain range. Finally, the satellite dish itself occupied the entire view. The shuttle banked towards its final descent and crew were pushed back into their seats as thrusters fired. The craft slowed until almost stopping above the landing field and the rear struts of the shuttle touched down. Maria fired bow thrusters and eased the nose onto the landing pad prepared by the Nyrians. The ship slowly fell forward until the front strut touched down. Quiet filled the cabin as she powered down the reactor.

They unbuckled and stood, taking places as agreed while aboard the *Sunspot*. Inessa waited by the door for the pressure to equalize and the locks to cycle open. Jardin took his place behind, followed by Shu Len, Ariana, Gunther and Maria. It was order based more on time in service than rank or role on the ship. Technically, Dave should have been standing by Jardin, maybe even in front. On sea-going ships, and on most in space, the person who kept the engines running was considered the captain's equal. As it was, he stood behind Alan, and he didn't mind. He shifted from foot to foot, testing out the gravity and giving his nerves an outlet through movement.

"Stand still," Eva said behind him, choosing her position because of the equipment she carried. "You're making me nervous."

"Aren't you already?" Dave asked.

"Of course, I am!" she said, "but you're making it worse." She set the case containing the translating devices down, finding them too heavy.

Alan listened to the two behind him, straightened his white tie and ran his fingers through his hair. Nyrians had hair. He knew that because Ceera told him. Two arms, two legs. Other similar parts. Whitman's verse asked questions Alan found himself too shy to ask for himself. She had a body, not too different from his own, that enjoyed being celebrated. He turned and looked at Eva, who, as communication specialist, was privy to almost all their conversations, a silent chaperone. Alan smiled as she caught his eye and then turned back to the door.

Inessa placed her hand on the latch and paused as if to speak. Final words of advice, guidance on conduct during the moments to follow. But she remained silent, breathed, exhaled slowly and opened the hatch. The seal popped and cool air rushed in. Everybody breathed deeply, eager to taste the new world. Inessa pushed the door open and stepped onto the ramp that extended from the shuttle. She glanced at the small crowd waiting below. Her eyes searched the forms below, letting her eyes be guided by instinct or ... she didn't know. They rested on a single form, male, very humanoid, and beautiful.

Beyond them the ringed gas giant filled almost a quarter of the sky. She reached out for the hand rail to steady herself as a wave of vertigo almost overwhelmed her. Focusing on the crowd, she willed herself forward, step by step. At the bottom of the ramp, she resisted the urge to touch the ground, to run her fingers over the strange grass, to feel an alien planet. Instead, she moved forward so her crew could form two lines behind her.

She looked over her shoulder and smiled at Jardin. He nodded and used his eyebrows to encourage her forward. She didn't need it. She was merely imprinting a moment into her synapses; one she knew she would never forget. She wanted to savor every detail. A crowd of Nyrians stood removed from the welcoming party, each talking intently into a microphone or recording device. *The ears of the world will be listening*, the Director told her. The staff from the radio dish stood in a small bunch, each peering at the crew from earth, searching faces, stopping and smiling when some sort of recognition was achieved. She glanced behind her and saw her crew doing the same.

As she moved forward, a single figure left the waiting Nyrians and walked towards her. The meeting was organized in an apparently casual manner that Inessa assumed was an aspect of Nyrian culture. An initial meeting, followed by the sharing of food, (which allowed the humans to sit while readjusting to gravity), a prepared speech to the waiting media, followed by a rest.

Inessa smiled as the Nyrian neared. The Director stopped and let Inessa approach. She stopped a meter in front of him and gazed into his eyes while breathing deeply.

"I invite you to know that I am open and receptive to knowing you," she said in words he could not understand. "That I see you," she said. Then she closed her eyes and bowed her head slightly as the Director told her it was done in his culture. She opened her eyes and met his again.

He, in turn, reciprocated the greeting, reaching out his hand as Inessa told him, in one of their many conversations from the ship, how it was done on earth. He took her hand in his and held it gently, before raising it and touching his lips to it. He continued to hold her hand, looked deeply into her eyes and said: "From the peoples of Nyria, and from myself, I welcome you to our home. I look forward to deepening our *union*."

Inessa was melting. Warmth spread through her chest. She smiled, a soft and open smile, beguiled, bewitched, by the man in front of her. Eva left her place in the front row of waiting crewmembers and approached with the case. The Director reluctantly released Inessa's hand and turned towards Eva, who held a translator bud in her fingers. She tilted her head from side to side and indicated her ear. The Director bent forward and stood still as Eva inserted the device into his ear. She returned to her place in line without a word.

"I see you," Inessa said. "And I am open and receptive."

The Director smiled in a manner not dissimilar to Inessa's. "I am honored. And I am gladdened. Come," he said, "let us sit and share sustenance."

Inessa and the Director moved towards a large table located beneath trees that seemed both familiar and strikingly different from any on earth. Leaves of the trees standing near stretched above to create shade, moving gently to maintain a canopy over the table. Alan searched among the Nyrians in the greeting party. His eyes rested on an individual standing in the second row, and her eyes met his. They both smiled at the same time. She started walking in his direction as her colleagues broke formation, all moving towards a human. Soon they stood before each other.

Ceera gazed into Alan's eyes and greeted him. She closed her eyes and bowed slightly, before meeting Alan's eyes again. She smiled.

"I invite you to know that I am open and receptive to knowing you, that I see you," Alan said, before closing his eyes and bowing. When he opened them again, he saw a small tear escape Ceera's eye.

The voice of the Director interrupted the greetings and the Nyrians turned to acknowledge him. Ceera took Alan's hand in hers and led him to the table, where they sat next to each other. Eva circulated among the group distributing ear buds, ensuring they were functional, before taking her seat next to Noor.

11

Alan touched his ear to turn off the translator device nestled there. Her voice was like operatic bird song, like wind through tall aspen, like—she playfully hit his hand and he lowered it.

"You're not even listening," she chastised, but there was no anger or disappointment in her tone, only amusement.

"I was listening," he protested. "You have the most beautiful voice."

She felt a softening warmth in the center of her chest in response to his smile. His blue eyes were open and inviting. Her hand stroked his arm. She knew he saw the same invitation in her eyes during the welcoming ceremony days past.

"You asked me about our transmitter, but I intuit you were wanting more understanding," she said.

He ran his fingers through blue grass, letting the soft blades tickle his fingers. The technology he had seen appeared to be purpose driven, unlike on Earth, where advances were made and exploited not because they were needed, but simply because they could. Or made to exploit resources under the ground or sea or deep in space. And worse, developed in times of war as ways to kill each other more efficiently. There was a lot he didn't want to tell her, that she didn't need to know, about how his own species used their inventiveness.

She could feel him hold back, and sensed defensiveness rather than deception. Perhaps, she admitted, there were things she didn't want or need to know right now. What he brought to her was wonderful. He was sitting beside her and giving freely of himself, if not needless details from his home. She felt the attraction as soon as she saw him, a glow among the small party that emerged from their ship. She touched him with her emotion and he glanced up, catching her eye, and he smiled.

"You call out to the stars, but don't try to go there," he said.

"The stars are here, beyond the sky, so why rush to them?" she teased. "Besides, they are so very far away, and there are more pressing things to do here."

"Like?"

"Like becoming. Like growing. Like expressing," she said. "Like loving. Isn't loving worth more energy than leaving?"

The way he bent his neck and turned to look—relaxed, smooth, tender. She felt the warmth in her heart descend lower.

"It is worth the energy," he said, nodding. "Loving."

"But you expended the effort to leave your home and come," she admitted, "and I am glad. We sent an invitation, and you answered. I am grateful. And I am pleased you came so quickly."

"We came after three hundred years!"

"No," she said. "You twisted time and space and came as soon as we called! Isn't that what your captain said?"

"Corkscrewed," he corrected. "She said we *corkscrewed* time."

"That word is too odd," she said. "I prefer twisting. It is like limbs wrapping themselves around each other in love making." She wriggled closer to him and put her leg over his, sliding her foot beneath his calf. She sensed a moment of hesitation with the closeness, but felt it fade away like smoke. He reached an arm around her and pulled her close and they lay down on the hillside. He felt an invisible point had been crossed, a fork in the road thus taken. He wanted to be with her, and silenced a voice within counseling ... he didn't care what it counseled anymore.

"We twisted time and space," he conceded, "so that I could meet you and hold you and smell you!" He buried his nose in her thick green hair and inhaled deeply. Then he released her and lay on his back beside her, gazing up at the giant ringed planet the moon orbited.

"Tell me how you did, how you came so quickly to me," she said, knowing he could not.

"I'm not a physicist!" he said. "I just study the air. The atmosphere."

"Same-same," she said. "Things you cannot see."

"Not same-same. One takes far more brains than I have. It's not my field."

"You have a beautiful and caring brain," she said, leaning on an elbow and stroking his soil-colored hair. Even his plain colors were beautiful. Eyes the color of sky, hair the color of soil, skin with so little color she could trace the veins beneath.

"Folding I understand. A and B. Fold space, put A and B together, and travel like that." She separated her thumb and middle finger. She brought her fingers together and snapped them.

He copied the motion, snapping his. "Just like that," he agreed. "There is a ship there now. Here, now. Or will be."

"Now you are not making sense," she said.

"Three hundred years from now a ship will visit Nyria, in response to your call. To see who is still here. My ship was tasked with responding to the first call, to see who sent the original message. You," he said.

"They are time travelers, voyaging to the future," Ceera said.

"No, we are the time travelers."

"But this is the present. The now," she said.

He knew their words were mere surface play, foreplay, but necessary. He felt a calmness in her presence that he lacked elsewhere in his life. Ambition, drive, desire to go or to be, painful memories or regrets, all dropped away. Simply being near her caused a calm and inner warmth that told him everything was as it should be, that there was no place else to be, except right here and right now and right next to her. Who traveled where and how were irrelevant. He turned and faced her. She glowed! She glowed ever since he felt her touch his mind, and he looked up and saw her among the welcoming group. Now he fell into her large emerald eyes.

"Okay, your time," she said, bringing him back to a hillside covered in blue grass, overlooking a slow-moving river, and farther in the distance, a radio transmitting station and a space ship.

"My time?" he asked.

"Three hundred years from now," she said. "When you were born. What does that make me, your grandmother?"

He sighed when she smiled. "A lot more than that," he said, trying to focus. "Right now, at this time, on my planet, ships only sail on the sea, not the air or in space. They are made from wood and use the wind to move across the water. I think we're just figuring out how to use machines to do that. But people still get around riding big animals called horses. It's all just terrible timing. When you called, we couldn't listen, and your message travelled three hundred lightyears, so even if we could—"

"As soon as you could you not only folded space, but you twisted time to see me," she said.

"Twisted it as hard as I could, to see you," he agreed. He stroked her cheek with his fingertips. Her skin was smooth and the color of ... raspberry sherbet, he decided, like the ice cream he enjoyed as a child. Such an amazing being! His chest swelled with gratitude that he was chosen for the *Response* ship rather than *Concurrent* contact. God only knows what that crew will find. *Response* was often merely a fly by, a record of what was, the secondary mission. Each time radio waves were detected that indicated sentient life through purposeful transmission, two ships were sent to investigate. *Response* was not meant to contact. But here they felt the attraction, each member of the crew, and they landed, and were greeted, and now ...

"I am so glad to be here," he said without thinking. "Here, with you. You are so beautiful. You make me feel ..."

"Like there is peace in the universe," she finished. "Like there is no other place to be. Like you spent your life as half of a person, and now you have found the other half. *Union*."

"Yes," he agreed, understanding more about the word.

She placed her hand on top of his, a gentle invitation. He turned his over and held hers, an acceptance. Her smile grew.

"Did you bring it?" she asked.

"Of course, I did," he answered.

"Then let me see!"

Alan opened the satchel he brought and withdrew a small book wrapped in cloth. He carefully opened the fabric and exposed the book hidden inside. He took it and handed it to Ceera. She held it as if it were made of thin glass, turning it over, studying its spine, and finally opening the cover to expose the pages within. The picture of the poet stared back at her, his shirt unbuttoned and his hat cocked jauntily to one side. She let out what Alan guessed was the Nyrian equivalent of a gasp.

"That is a picture of him as a young man," Alan said. "This is a reproduction of the first edition. See," he added, touching his finger to numbers at the bottom of the page. "That says, '1855'. It is the year when he published it."

"Years from now," Ceera said.

"Yes," Alan said softly, noticing that they were whispering.

"Will you read to me?" Ceera asked.

"Of course," Alan answered. "I marked some passages." He opened the book to the first section. "This part is my favorite," he said. "It is titled: *I Sing the Body Electric*."

"Read to me," Ceera said, resting her head against Alan's chest and closing her eyes.

"The bodies of men and women engirth me, and I engirth them. They will not let me off nor I them till I go with them and respond to them and love them.

"The expression of the body of man or woman balks account, the male is perfect and that of the female is perfect.

"The expression of a wellmade man appears not only in his face, it is in his limbs and joints also ... it is curiously in the joints of his hips and wrists,

Ceera snuggled closer as Alan paused to locate another passage.

"This is the female form," he continued.

"It attracts with fierce undeniable attraction,

"I am drawn by its breath as if I were no more than a helpless vapor .... all falls aside but myself and it.

"Hair, bosom, hips, bend of legs, negligent falling hands—all diffused .... Mine too diffused,

"Limitless limpid jets of love hot and enormous .... Quivering jelly of love .... White-blow and delirious juice,

"Bridegroom-night of love working surely and softly into the prostrate dawn,

"Undulating into the willing and yielding day,

"Lost in the cleave of the clasping and sweetfleshed day."

Alan stopped reading and took a deep breath. Ceera rose to her knees and took the book. She folded it carefully back into its cloth protection and put it into the satchel.

"Come," she said, taking his hand.

And they stood and she guided him down a neatly groomed path to the bottom of the hill where a tidy row of small houses stood. She led him up the front stairs to her home, and only released his hand once they were inside. She placed a hand on each of his shoulders and looked up into his eyes, and his hands found her hips. Their bodies vibrated with anticipation.

"Let us join," she said softly, and he followed her to the bedroom.

They undressed slowly in front of each other, both smiling, both mesmerized. She touched his bare chest, the dark hairs that covered his strong muscles. Such an exquisite creature, she thought in wonder. Her hand passed over his stomach, firmly rounded his hip until wrapping itself around his member. She could feel his body tremble. He gently cupped her breast, lifting it, bending and kissing her nipple, tasting it with his tongue. His other hand ran down her back, until it reached her bottom. She felt his energy increase, felt his urge to lose control.

He would need guidance. She stepped slightly back. "Lie down," she instructed.

He obeyed, lying on the bed. She stepped over and straddled him. Reaching between her legs, she moistened her fingers and rubbed them on his tip. Then she slowly lowered herself, guiding him into her agonizingly slowly. When he tried to raise up to meet her, she pressed him down, controlling the penetration. When he was deep inside her, she sat motionless, gripping him tightly with her thighs.

"Look at me," she said, and his eyes travelled up her belly and her breasts and her neck and met her gaze. "Stay with the energy, our energy," she said.

She started to massage him from within, a gentle pulsing that urged him to explode, but each time he reached the precipice, she slowed herself and held him as close to the edge as he could bear, increasingly building the energy between them. She breathed deeply in through her nose and exhaled slowly from her mouth, in rhythm with her womanhood, and soon he breathed with her, until they became one breath, one energy, one light, one being. After what felt like a moment, or an hour, or an eternity, she placed a hand on the middle of his chest and closed her eyes and he knew it was permission to climax.

They lay together in her bed as the day began to fade into the slightly dimmer time that the earthlings referred to as 'night'. Soft light filtered through the window. His mind began to wonder, to fantasize about bringing her home, how lonely she might feel, how alien. He dreamed of staying with her, on this world, the only member of his species. Could he fit in? Could he leave everything behind? He gazed at her resting face. Her eyes were closed and she breathed softly. He knew she wasn't asleep. Maybe she was thinking similar thoughts. Maybe she, too, wanted to just push them aside, to be in this moment, this wonderful moment. He closed his eyes and surrendered to what he knew as the only truth. That he loved the being lying beside him.

They lay in bed resting while time slipped by unnoticed. Finally, she rose and went into the small kitchenette, returning with two glasses of water. Alan took his and drank, draining the glass.

"Slowly, my love," Ceera told him. "Everything slowly."

She took the glass from his hand and set it on the small table beside the bed. She sipped from her own, set her glass down and wiped her lips with the back of her fingers. She pulled the sheets back, revealing her lover's body. She smiled as it responded. He didn't need that much rest. She climbed onto the bed and sat between his legs, pushing his knees apart. Bending forward, she flicked her tongue over the tip of his member.

"Take a moment and relax," she said. "Close your eyes with me and come into your body. Feel your body."

She sat and crossed her legs, breathed deeply, and closed her eyes.

"With every exhalation," she said, "relax a little more. Exhale ... inhale." She breathed in between words, expecting him to follow her example. "As you exhale, contract your pelvic floor. Inhale, and then relax your muscles there." Ceera touched herself between her legs, pressing the muscle between her vagina and anus. She opened her eyes and saw Alan watching her. She reached towards him and placed her hands under his testicles, to his perineum, and pushed.

"Right there," she said. "Feel that area as you exhale. Clench those muscles. This will help you control your urge to release. Now, inhale ... relax. Exhale ...contract. It is cyclical. In and out. Focus on your perineum as you exhale, contract, and then follow the breath upwards as you inhale, through your body, through your heart, and then out your mouth."

She sat in front of him, legs crossed and smiling. He drew up his legs and sat facing her. She closed one eye, a gesture he explained was called a wink, but she did it slowly. He fought back a giggle. He closed his eyes as she did.

"Exhale and contract," she said. "Imagine the energy going down, all the way to the tip of your penis, and then exhale and contract and let the energy flow upwards, through your head. I am doing the same, I am with you, and the energy flows throughout our bodies. Feel it, burning at your manhood, and exhale, letting the energy flow upwards."

She breathed several times. "Stay in your body for now," she said without opening her eyes. After several minutes, she moved closer to him, climbing onto his lap. She felt his member against her, reached down and lifted it, placing it against her belly.

"This time breathe through me," she instructed. "Send your energy through me, as if you were penetrating me. Send your energy into me. Let your breath be just as your beautiful manhood. When you inhale, take in my energy. It burns within me, burns within my groin, this powerful energy. I feel it, I feel it's urge, and I send it to you, up through my body through my breasts and into your chest. Take it, take it deep, take me deep within, and let my energy flow downwards, through your chest, through your torso, into your sex, and exhale. When you breath out, let the energy flow into me, into my body and through my womanhood."

She lifted herself slightly, took him in her hand and guided him inside. She sat down slowly, taking him deep within. "Feel the energy flow, creating a circle, uniting the two of us. Inhale. Feel the energy of your sex, its heat, its power. Chanel that power. Chanel it through my body, your energy mixing with mine, and exhale. Give it to me. Fill me with the energy. Feel everything, Alan. Feel my heat. Feel my moisture. Feel my love. Feel your intensity. Feel how it throbs, how it yearns, how it wants to explode and experience eternity. But do not explode. Stay with the power. Exhale and connect. Send your passion to me, through you, and into me, until it is all there is, a golden circle of our light. Receive my passion, my energy. Take it all in. Breathe, Alan. Breathe with me. Exhale. Contract all those muscles. Inhale. Stay with me.

"Do not think of the ending," she breathed into his ear. "The urge is great, but don't focus on an end goal. Be in this moment. Together, in this moment. Inhale. Feel everything. Exhale."

Alan tried to focus on his breath, on his body, on his genitals, on Ceera's body, on her genitals ... in the end he lost focus.

"Stay with me," she whispered. "You can move. That's it. I can feel every inch of you. Slowly. There is no hurry. There is nowhere to go. There is just right now. Yes, Alan. Be with me for every moment. Feel every moment."

Alan found his awareness at several places at once. He breathed and felt Ceera breathe. He moved and felt Ceera respond. He turned her over and lay on top of her. He slowed down, entering her gradually, feeling her take him. He savored each moment, his mind becoming concentrated on each sensation, merging and melting with that part of his body. He entered as far he could go, and he let her hold him. Moments turned into minutes as they breathed together. Finally, he felt her smile against his cheek. Her lips found his ear lobe and she bit it.

"How do we know when to stop?" he asked.

"We don't ever have to stop," she breathed into his ear.

"That's good," he answered.

12

Alan and Ceera walked for hours, leaving the messaging station and the ship behind. They followed a path through the forest, branches seemingly moving out of the way in a very un-earthlike way. As first twilight approached, they crossed a low saddle in the hills and lost site of the station. The translator device could not easily find a word to describe this time, when the light of the daytime sun dimmed and the world was lit by the reflection of the giant rings and refracted light from below the gas giant's horizon, making the massive planet above appear closer, threatening to fall and crush the small moon. Could it be called twilight if no dark followed? Alan mused. A twilight appears in the lower atmosphere, whereas the entire sky was aglow on Nyria during the 'night'. There was never a real night as Alan understood it. Only during eclipse did the sky truly reveal the many stars in the darkness of space.

Alan turned off the translator device and made Ceera say the word describing this time of day several times, preferring it to any translation. He tried to repeat it and she laughed. Eva told him it was not physically possible to speak Nyrian as humans did not possess a syrinx, which held Nyrian vocal cords deeper in their bodies, nor did they have the two sets of vocal cords that enabled Nyrians to make two different sounds simultaneously.

"Come, there is a special place I want to show you," she said, taking his hand.

He walked beside her to the top of the rise where she stopped and sat down. Alan sat near and followed her gaze across a lush valley that was once the caldera of long extinct super volcano, ending at a range of mountains that rose in the east. Ceera nudged him playfully when she saw him smiling.

"See?" she asked. "Same-same. My mountains on the horizon, like your mountains on your horizon."

"Same-same," he answered.

He had seen them through the eyes of his probes, knew how many kilometers they ran, knew their altitude (higher than the Sierras back home) but the view from this hillock, shared with the woman sitting next to him, took his breath away.

"They are very beautiful," he added, turning.

"You are not looking at them," she said.

"You are beautiful," he said. "Thank you for bringing me here." He leaned over and kissed her, his lips lightly touching hers, lingering, and opening fuller. Finally, she placed a hand on his chest and felt his heart beating. Their faces parted and when their eyes opened, they saw the other smiling.

She pointed towards the mountains. "The cabin is over there. After the tour, at *hiemal*, we can go there to share the night. It is a magical place. And *hiemal* is an intimate time. It will be a dream come true." She took his hand.

"That will be nice," Alan said, feeling the inadequacy of his response.

The translator selected a close match to something both concrete and ephemeral. He looked at the mountains again, his eyes running along the summit of the range. There is no snow, he thought. In a world with no real night, snow and ice did not linger even at the higher elevations. And yet every three years Nyria was swallowed in the shadow of the gas giant and darkness and cold blanketed the world for months. *Hiemal*: of the winter, of all things wintry. From Ceera's description of the triennial event, the word choice was inadequate in describing the occasion. The change was the paramount event in the Nyrian calendar, a natural occurrence that shaped their culture, their understanding of the place of their species in the wider cosmos. *The time when the goddess rested.* A time when the planet seemed to rest, cloaked in a mantel of snow. There had been no discussion yet about 'wintering over' on Nyria. There had been little of any discussion beyond the tour, as each team member explored their relationship with their Nyrian *liaison*.

But Alan understood that what Ceera was asking was more than an invitation to visit a cabin in the mountains. *We can go there to share the night.* The translator was useless in conveying deeper cultural meaning. Alan looked at Ceera and felt a calm warmth spread throughout his body, a response he was growing used to. *That would be nice*, was not an appropriate response. He wondered how it translated, and knew he would need to help those words.

"I have something for you," Alan said. He reached into his satchel and withdrew a small rectangle wrapped in cloth. "I want you to have this."

"No!" she said.

"It is a gift, for you," Alan answered. "Something I want you to have."

She took it gingerly from him, turning it in her hand and examining the cloth. She was confused. The translator failed her as it did Alan in deciphering cultural meanings. She realized that his giving was too layered for her to completely grasp.

"You open it," Alan said. "Unwrap the cloth. The gift is inside. It is what we do when we give. We usually wrap them colorful paper. Or pieces of cloth, if we happen to be on a planet without wrapping paper."

She placed the parcel on her lap and stroked the cloth, unsure how to proceed in this new cultural experience. "This is your ... I cannot. It is part of you."

"It's okay," Alan reassured. "I'm giving it to you. Now you must open it. It's yours."

Ceera turned it over and lifted a piece of cloth. She uncovered more of the parcel, ceremoniously lifting another piece, and another, until the volume hidden inside was revealed. Cooing escaped from her throat. She lifted the book as if it were an injured bird and held it in both hands.

"No, Alan," she said, gazing at it. "This is too valuable. You must keep it."

She turned towards him and offered it, but he closed his hands around hers and pushed it softly back. "It is yours now. I want you to have it," he said.

Tears formed and flowed down her cheeks. She was not used to showing emotion, but with Alan it felt safe. "I cannot read it," she said.

"I will read it to you."

"It is too valuable. It is too special," she protested.

"That is why I want you to have it," Alan said.

Ceera leaned into Alan's chest and he wrapped his arms around her. She shuddered slightly as she cried. Alan gave her a moment before drawing back. He took the book from her and opened it to a page that had a diagonal line across the top where it had been folded numerous times to mark a place. Faint pencil marked the page.

"This is my favorite line, right here," he said. "See that line, and the words above it. I wanted it to be easy to find, but I have long since memorized it. I like to think it is what he ... I ..."

"Read it to me," Ceera said.

Alan took a breath. He plucked a piece of grass from where they sat. "See? It's what he is looking at on the cover. A leaf of grass."

"*Leaves of Grass*," she said. "The title."

"Yes," he agreed. "It's simple, really. But beautiful. A simple leaf of grass, containing the entire universe." Alan ran his finger along the marked line. "He writes: *I believe a leaf of grass is no less than the journey work of the stars*."

"He saw love everywhere," Ceera said.

"It is everywhere," Alan said.

"And he felt *union* with it," Ceera added.

She leaned into him and he put his arm around her. She listened as he read and the distant mountains became illuminated by reflected light.

Ceera never met her mother. At least, not as Alan would have understood. She was, no doubt, among the many carers at the creches where she was weaned and raised. When she moved with her age cohort to a young infant center, the woman who birthed her would have gone onto another domicile and continued her life. Ceera knew many carers as 'mother' and 'father'. All the adults around her were her parents, just as all the children she lived with were her siblings.

As Ceera grew, her domiciles changed. After entering pubescence, she lived in a large domicile with her own bed and privacy curtain.

It wasn't considered as such. Privacy was not a concept understood by Nyrians. Most of the time the curtain was just decorative vestments in a shared space. Everything was shared. As her body changed and matured, it was also shared with the others in her domicile, equally intrigued and excited by what was happening within them. When they were younger, the children preferred to crowd into each other's space and snuggle for warmth and security and comfort. As the young Nyrians grew, they lifted the flimsy curtains between their beds and explored the pleasures of encroaching adulthood. For Ceera, these were intense moments of connection. When she was younger, her favorites were her domicile sisters, Ceera pleasuring as she liked being pleasured, feeling whole for as long as their ecstasy lasted.

Afterward, and alone in her bed, she felt what it meant to be truly alone. She initially thought it was the price to pay for such intense connection, a consequence of closeness, to be left feeling empty, emptied, different, alien. She willingly paid that price, because she thought those around her similarly paid. Her spectrum of thought did not permit a different interpretation of what she was feeling. It was simply not possible to think otherwise.

And then she discovered the pleasure of the opposite sex. She shared with one boy, Tumi, opening her mind and body to new experiences. She cherished how it felt as she slipped out of her bed, gently pushed aside the curtain, and crept into his bed. He was the first to enter her, to join in closeness deep within. Other boys shared with her, in what was, to her and the youth around, the normal way of things. But when she thought of Tumi, his image brought an additional warmth. One night she crept out of her curtained area, wet with anticipation and yearning, and tip toed to Tumi's bed. Only, as she neared, she heard heavy breathing and the creak of his bed as he shared with another. She returned to her own bed, and was joined shortly after by another boy. She could not remember that sharing, only the feeling of ... She did not have a word to describe it, just the image of burrowing under the ground. Not the digging itself, but the hollow cavern left behind.

That feeling was nothing compared to the look he gave her days later, when he caught her sneaking glances during lessons, or found her staring, as if in a dream, during meals. She wanted to consume him with her eyes, to bring him within, to hold him, to revel in the warmth of his existence. He saw her and he flinched, as if he stepped in something unpleasant. He was repulsed by her advances. How could a face convey so much just by the movement of a few muscles? A quick reflex passed across his face and Ceera was crushed by the weight of shame and guilt and loneliness.

It was loneliness that drove her away when she finally reached maturity. Paradoxically, being alone was less painful than being lonely among others. Those around her could not fail to notice her difference. While they blossomed around her, she became obscured in a dark cloud. The adults around her treated the young melancholic with therapy. When talk did not brighten her mood, they tried medications, as well as experimental treatments including electrical jolts to her frontal cortex. The sessions left her feeling even more empty, only capable of wandering about the domicile quietly, smiling. That seemed to please those around her, or so she thought. When she overheard operative procedures being discussed, she gathered her personal possessions, which, like most Nyrians, were the clothes on her back, and she left the collective.

Ceera caught an airship to a nearby city and blended into anonymity. She studied broadcasting and joined a domicile group. She applied herself to the needs of the commune, sharing everything she had, as expected, until her pain pushed her out. She drifted across the continent on the winds, just as the airships that carried her. Ceera met Noor by accident. She missed a transport and waited at the deserted port for the next airship. She sat by herself, as she became too used to doing, preferring solitude to the loneliness of the crowd, and he sat next to her. They were the only two passengers in the entire hangar. There were hundreds of other seats, but he took the one next to her. He looked at her and he smiled. He said words that no healthy, or *normal*, Nyrian would, or perhaps could, say.

"Airports are such lonely places," he said. "They are so much worse when they are crowded. But when they are empty they are almost bearable."

Ceera never knew where Noor was heading that day, but they traveled together since their meeting. In the domiciles they shared a bed, but not each other, sleeping close so others would not join them. As those around began to notice the odd behavior of this odd pair, Ceera and Noor moved on. To another city, another domicile. They became something new to each other, a word the earthling's translating device chose to label 'friend'. Together they formed a connection, one that provided comfort, but that did not reach the depth they both craved. They would never form *union*. And although that was what each sought, they were comforted by the relationship they had.

And then one day by accident, or serendipitously or by some predestined plan, they heard the story of a crazed scientist dreaming of talking to the stars, of reaching past the goddess (who provided for all needs) and broadcasting an invitation into the unknown. They made their way to the remote location where he worked, as did others they would soon also be known as 'friends' and 'family', where they built a large dish and radio tower to broadcast their message. When Ceera and Noor arrived, they did not find a dangerous lunatic, or deranged hermit, or an existential threat to the collective, as the media portrayed. They merely found another lonely and incomplete individual like themselves.

13

Alan relaxed into his seat as the airship gained altitude. Ceera's hand lay over the arm rest, cupped in his own. He looked up the isle and saw other crew sitting similarly, with their Nyrian counterpart beside them, hands together or heads resting on the other's shoulder. It had been several days since Alan had seen his *Sunspot* colleagues. His captain, Inessa, sat at the front, her forehead resting against the Director's. Alan furled his brow, trying to remember his name, accessing imaginary files in his mind. For so many days, he had only thought of the feel and the musky scent of the woman next to him, shutting off any distraction during their ... what did Ceera call it? A time after their welcome, when they could relax and recuperate, get to know each other. The translator had difficulty with the word used by the Nyrians. Something that made Alan think of his Catholic childhood. Their *retreat*? Their *Communion*?

Let us join, she had said.

"Tauma," Alan said under his breath, trying to replicate the sound of the name in Nyrian. He looked from the Director and his captain, then to Eva, who smiled as she sat next to Noor, and to Shu Len, sitting beside Daan, her Nyrian partner, sharing a quiet aside. Shu Len laughed at a comment or joke Alan could not hear. He looked around the cabin. Twelve travelers from earth meeting twelve radio technicians from a distant planet. Alan watched Gunther gently stroke the cheek of the Nyrian next to him. Her name was Hylua. Gunther looked relaxed. Happy. No. He looked like a man in love.

And Jardin couldn't keep his hands off his ... *liaison*. The word was another of those the translator had difficulty with precision when it came to meaning. A liaison is a contact or a communication. It was a word that could be both noun and adjective. It sounded almost impersonal, like affiliate, associate, contact, partner. But on Nyria, they were much more. They *communed*. That was a better word, Alan thought, but it was still lacking. It carried with it an intimacy and intensity, a sharing of something more than words. He gave up, admitting that what he tried to describe was perhaps beyond words.

Alan stroked Ceera's hand, thinking he understood the word a little better. Dave sat beside his Nyrian contact. Alan couldn't remember her name. He spent the last few days forgetting many names of people who were over three hundred lightyears away, people not even born yet, unhurt by him, or yet to cause him pain. Slights or phrases from his past, even those that were said (*I just don't feel it anymore*) seemed insignificant. During the recent days, his every thought seemed to be about the one person whose hand he was holding.

Alan tilted his head and met Ceera's eyes. She smiled softly; her head nestled against the soft seatback. Airships travelled slowly, and voyages took time, so Nyrians made their vessels comfortable. He returned her smile.

"What are you thinking about?" she asked him.

He looked over, remembering they were floating above the surface of an alien world.

"You," he said. "Your smell. And taste. And feel. And ..."

She placed a hand on his thigh and squeezed, and tilted her head back. "That is good," she said. "Continue to think."

She held the copy of *Leaves of Grass* on her lap, running her fingers over the image on the cover. The young poet lay on a grassy bank, head supported by a hand. His shirt was open at the chest and his hat cocked to one side. In his other hand he held a leaf of grass, and he studied it intensely. She opened the book to the only other illustration: Whitman, standing, one hand on hip and the other in his pocket. She gently touched the chin of the figure. Both pictures were painted by the American artist, Lewis C. Daniel. *No, he didn't pose for the artist. They never met ... How? He must have used a photograph, an image ... A photograph. It's a still image, preserved on paper, like a drawing but ...* Alan had a momentary regret, wishing he had brought an illustrated edition, but none held his heart as this one, an old paperback copy found in a used book store that he carried with him for years, and across space. But she was delighted. The words on the pages were mere scratches to Ceera, an indecipherable script, so she returned frequently to the cover, and the only image inside. The volume had not left her since he gave it to her, and it bound them closer: she the holder of words and he the interpreter of meaning.

Dave rose from his seat, walked up the aisle and patted Alan's shoulder as he passed. He tilted his head towards the viewing lounge at the stern of the gondola. Ceera squeezed Alan's leg again before giving it a gentle push. She smiled and moved her head in the direction of his colleague.

"Join him, I will nap now," Ceera said.

Alan kissed her cheek before rising and joining Dave in the lounge. He sighed as he sank into the cushioned chair, and swiveled to face the large windows. Several airships followed behind, making a silent procession over the river below. After covering their every public move, and exhausting them with their own interviews, the media were now in train to their next appearance. Sometime during the next day, their airship would moor at the largest city on Nyria, where three million residents waited. Press conferences, public engagements, official visits. The usual land-based work routine, with a very unusual intensity. A steward offered a tray with drinks and Alan took one.

"This is a lovely way to travel," he said, still gazing out the window.

"Not if you're in a hurry," Dave said without turning.

"Are you in a hurry?"

"Not at all," Dave said. "But it's nice to be moving."

"I have mixed feeling about that," Alan said. "I thought it was pleasant at the station."

"That's rather obvious," Dave said. "You look drugged. High. But in a good way."

"It feels pretty good," Alan responded. "Aren't you enjoying time with your *liaison*?"

"Enjoy?" Dave answered. "That is too mild a word. The sex ... my god," he said, lowering his voice. "Mind blowing."

He looked up and checked they were alone in the lounge. Noticing Alan's drink for the first time he motioned to the steward, who returned with another. Dave sipped it when they were alone again, staring out the window with Alan. The ever-present gas giant hung in the sky. An inner moon orbited above the rings.

"It's all very intense," Dave said.

"Agreed. Don't you like it?"

"Of course, I like it," Dave said. "Salia is wonderful. It's just that ... I'm used to working alone, spending a lot of time alone, just me and the reactor and all that goes with keeping her humming. Down here ... I mean, she's ... it's all rather intense. Like being drugged."

"And again, don't you like it?"

"To be honest, not all the time," Dave said. "I like having a clear mind. Being focused. It's what I love about my work. The reactor demands focus. Now, all I can think about is her. It's intense. Quit smiling at me like that." He took a drink and wiped his mouth with the back of his hand. "Everybody is acting like they're high all the time. I mean, check out Gunther. He has a wife and two kids back in Germany. That doesn't seem to matter to him here. And Inessa." Dave shook his head and took a deep breath. "That woman is in love. Hell, you're in love. You and ... I'm sorry, what's her name?"

"Ceera," Alan answered. "And he's separated. Gunther. It was pretty acrimonious from what I can gather. Not that it's any of our business."

"Well, you and Ceera are inseparable." Dave leaned closer and lowered his voice. "And Salia, I think she's in love. Hell, I might be in love. I don't know what I'm feeling. It's all way too intense."

"Maybe you need to slow down a bit," Alan said.

"That's a stupid thing to say," Dave shot back. He placed a hand on Alan's arm. "Sorry, man," he quickly added. "Things *are* moving way too fast. Unlike this airship."

"It's a good speed," Alan said. He took Dave's hand before the other man could withdrawal it. "Talk to me. What's going on?" he asked.

Dave looked towards the compartment holding the other passengers, then placed his free hand over Alan's. "I'm good," he said. "I could use a drink, that's for sure."

"You're not the only one, But I don't think there's too much of that on the planet. Not that I've come across, anyway."

"I know where there's a little flask of Scotch whiskey," Dave said, "but it's orbiting above us at the moment. Smuggled on board and hidden in a certain reactor technician's quarter."

"It'll still be ther.,"

"I know," Dave said. "It's just … I don't want to lead these people on. We're not going to be here forever," he added after a moment. "I like them. I like Salia."

"But?" Alan asked.

"But I need some space." Dave shifted in his seat, as if physically pressed in on both sides.

"Have you asked for it? Space?" Alan asked.

"How would that feel?" Dave said. "A person wants to be with you, and you tell them to back off."

"It doesn't have to come out like that. Just tell her you need a bit of time each day to collect yourself. Recharge. Whatever."

"How would anybody not take that as a rejection?" Dave asked. "Hey, I like you, but I need to get away from you for a while." Dave sat silently for a moment before speaking again. "I feel like I've had somebody next to me every minute after the welcoming."

"Just ask for it. She'll understand," Alan said.

"And we're just visiting, man. Aren't we? Everybody seems to have forgotten that."

"No," Alan said. "I don't think we've forgotten. We just don't want to think about it." He gazed up the aisle to where Ceera sat, her hair showing between the seats. He felt like he was lying to his crewmate. Or lying to himself.

"That's part of the problem," Dave said. "Even Inessa won't talk about it. She's not being a leader when we need one. And this winter thing is coming up—"

"*Heimal*," Alan said.

"Yeah. An eclipse that lasts months. More months away from the ship," Dave said. "And everybody seems totally okay with that."

"Ceera invited me to spend it with her," Alan said. "I don't see what the problem is. What is with the rush to return topside? It isn't going anywhere. The ship is secure."

"Never mind," Dave said.

"Hey, I mind," Alan said. "You can talk to me. I admit I've been distracted."

They gazed out the windows for a few moments before Alan spoke again. "You haven't experienced a tour before, so I should let you know, they can be a little on the busy side."

"So I've heard," Dave said.

"You might have heard," Alan said. "But experiencing is different. It's like being in a band on tour, everywhere you go, folks wanting a piece of you. God only knows what it'll be like as alien rock stars. If you need some Dave time, you'll need to carve it out. Even if she doesn't understand, she'll give it to you."

14

Deckhands threw out rings attached to thick line from the bow and stern of the airship as it descended over what may have been a park in the Nyrian city. Rectangular, grey buildings radiated outward from the central green space. Each building resembled a shoe box, either standing upright or laying on its side, reflecting a utilitarian rather than an artistic design. Ground crew standing on platforms hanging on poles planted in the soil caught the rings and slid them over the anchor posts, tethering the front and back of the ship. Releasing a mechanism, their platform slid slowly down the pole until they could hop off and join others on the ground catching lines thrown from the gondola. They attached the lines to winches, and the lines grew taught as the machines grabbed them.

The passengers above felt a jolt as the winches pulled the airship down towards the blue grass below. When it was two meters from the ground, the winches stopped and the lines made fast. Groundcrew pushed a ramp to the gondola and secured it both above and below before the doors were opened. Inessa and Tauma led the party out of the airship and down the ramp. The others followed in their pre-arranged places. Alan nudged Ceera and smiled as he gazed up at the buildings surrounding the airfield, or park, or whatever function the place played in the city. He didn't notice Ceera's lack of a smile as she returned to a place she already knew.

Eva scanned the surroundings from her place in line behind them, the camera in her glasses taking in the scene. Those waiting for them below already wore translator buds, sent ahead of the party, and leaving Eva free to act in her expanded role of secret film maker, capturing the culture of their hosts through a technology they didn't understand. She felt the need to scratch the itch at the back of her mind that questioned the ethics of what she was doing. But what she was recording was too exciting to lift that hand. People back home would go crazy over the images, and she realized she was pioneering a new field. She tried to find a word for what she was doing, none quite capturing it. Exo-ethnolinguist? Exo-anthropologist? *Spy*, the itch at the back of her head offered.

Eva stared ahead and filmed everything. A large crowd framed the scene unfolding below the city's tallest buildings. The line of dignitaries straightened as Inessa neared them. Behind them stood what on earth would be considered an honor guard, each holding what on either planet would be taken as weapons. Eva twitched her nose and zoomed on the devices. They were long barreled like a rifle, slung from shoulders by a wide strap. At the end were two cylinders. She blinked several times and took still images of the devices for examination later before moving her gaze back to the ceremony. The dignitary stood before an array of microphones that separated he and Inessa. He droned on, saying words Eva was certain they would hear at every city visited. Eva zoomed in on Inessa, who smiled patiently and gave the man one hundred percent of her attention. She was good at this, Eva admitted.

The dignitary finished his speech and bowed slightly. Inessa waited a moment before responding. Her words were similar to her first address, hand reaching out across the stars and all that. Inessa bent closer to the mics and made her speech. Eva worked with some of the Nyrian media before they left and was proud of her improvised engineering with the devices. As Inessa spoke, the listeners in their homes heard an almost instantaneous translation of her words into their language. It was another protocol bent or broken—handing over advanced technology. It was an offering, of sorts, displaying an openness that was not really there.

The watching crowd made a trilling noise when Inessa finished, that the translating device refused to recognize as speech. Eva focused on a small group making the sound and fought the reflex to nod when she understood it was the equivalent of applause. Inessa waved to the crowd, and the city dignitary led the party into the building acting as the backdrop to the grand display. Food, followed by a rest at their quarters, followed by a word loosely translated to *party*.

The honor guard behind the dignitaries parted and formed two lines that funneled the group into the reception center. The city official leading the welcome offered his hand and Inessa took it. She stepped forward with him into the building. Tauma walked behind them, flanked by another from the greeting party. Inessa glanced behind at her *liaison*, and he nodded his ascent. Chen followed Inessa, walking in front of Bourtul. As the procession continued to form, each of the astronauts were separated from their Nyrian partner. Alan placed his left arm around Ceera's waist, determined to keep her next to him. When his official escort extended a hand to lead him on, Ceera pulled lightly away and he tightened his hold on her hip. He placed his right hand on the Nyrian' shoulder.

"I thank you, my friend," Alan said. "And I acknowledge you. Let's follow the others." He guided the man gently with his hand still on his shoulder, giving him no choice but to walk with them, three abreast.

Eva smiled from behind, entwining her arm in Noor's. When her host approached, she offered her other arm, and the carefully choreographed entrance fell apart as those behind formed more of a loose line of couples and guides.

Inside the reception hall, Inessa stood beside a large table speaking with the city official. She pointed to a smaller table nearby with twelve chairs around it. The official replied and Inessa shook her head. Eva could see the captain's smile, one her crew instantly recognized, but there was no way the Nyrian could read the nuance of the expression. After a moment of silence, the official understood a little better. He waved a hand and issued an order. Servers emerged to move chairs and pull the second table to the first, then rearrange all the seats around both. Inessa's smile grew warmer and more genuine. The dignitary pulled out a chair, then a second, indicated, and she and Tauma sat down. Once all were sitting around the two joined tables, the food arrived.

While still at their small settlement, Ceera played Nyrian music for Alan, and he politely listened. There were many types of music on earth he didn't quite get or enjoy. The sharp nasality of Chinese folk music, pop music of any stripe, improvised jazz, or so called 'contemporary' classical music. The latter sounded to Alan like putting a cat in garbage can and tossing it down a flight of stairs. Call it what you will, labelling that 'music' was a long stretch. The music Ceera played in her little house was not as abrasive as cats in a can, or as self-indulgent as jazz off the cuff (as if "Johnny-O on the bass!" being announced after ten minutes of plucking made it okay), but he didn't quite 'get' it. He smiled and nodded at the right time, feigning enjoyment, just as he imagined she would have had he played a recording of his favorite acoustic solo.

Standing in the wide reception room, illuminated with shifting colored lights, Alan started to sway with the strange rhythm buried deep in the sounds. Ceera moved closer, her hips brushing his as she swayed. He followed her lead and began to bend like a tree in the wind, first to the left and then slowly to the right. He felt Ceera's breath, warm against his cheek, her chest against his. Their bodies became one. He sighed, and a little moan escaped, ticking Ceera's ear. She began to lean forward and Alan leaned back to accommodate, their bodies growing closer, then they swayed with the sounds.

As the music faded, Ceera moved slower until they were standing close together. She stepped away and Alan noticed the others in the room, as if they had materialized from vapor.

"Wow," Alan said.

He felt a presence next to him and a woman from the greeting party placed a hand on his shoulder. He saw she wasn't wearing a translator bud, but thought he knew what she was asking. Alan glanced at Ceera.

"She wants to dance with you," Ceera said. "You are free to do so."

Alan smiled at the Nyrian, lifted a hand and touched her cheek. "I am sorry," he said, "but I am dancing with Ceera."

The Nyrian tilted her head in a fashion he had seen Ceera do when she did not quite grasp meaning of what he said or did. With the woman standing in front of him, he wasn't sure if it was confusion or a bewildered disdain. Alan turned and took Ceera's hand, gesturing to himself and to Ceera with the other. The Nyrian woman tilted her head to the other side with the same expression before walking back into the crowd. Alan stepped closer to Ceera and the music grew louder again.

Across the floor, Maria felt a hand on her shoulder as she separated from Nola. She turned and smiled at the man, a rainbow flashing on his face as the colored lights illuminated his skin. He leaned slowly to the right and Maria understood.

"I think he wants to dance," she said to Nola.

"You are free to do so," Nola answered, the ingrained response escaping before she could stop or change it.

Maria kissed Nola on the cheek before turning toward the man, who moved closer as a new set of sounds filled the room. He swayed slowly against her and she bent with him. He closed the space between them, feeling her chest and thighs against his own. She felt his manhood stiffening against her and she grew excited at the contact in the crowded room. She felt another presence behind her, hands stroking her thighs as a body, most definitely male, pressed against her from behind. The two swayed with Maria willingly trapped between, as the lights began to follow sound and their entwined bodies melded with the sensory display around them.

As the music finally faded, she felt wet with sweat and lust. She shook her head in an attempt to clear it. Her two partners stepped back, but remained touching in some way—a hand on her hip, her wrist gently cupped in another's hand. She looked for Nola, but her Nyrian partner retreated during the dance to another area of the floor, and stood beside Cartan whose partner, Jardin, also danced with others. Maria felt the fingers of third Nyrian gently touch her cheek, and the three became four as more sound played and another dance began. When the music finally faded, her pulse raced and her legs felt weak. She leaned against one of her partners, scanning the room again for Nola, finding her near the rear of the room.

Maria felt herself guided off the dance floor and towards an exit door. She tried to stop walking with the others, before they left the room. With the small amount of resistance she could muster, she pushed off her guide and stood uneasily on her own. One reached an inviting hand and she weakly pushed it away.

"Thank you," she said, both palms facing her dance partners, her words mere guttural barks to the ears of the Nyrians. "Thank you," she repeated. "That was ... but I must return to my colleagues."

A Nyrian reached out again, this time slowly, palm facing up, inviting. He stopped before touching her, indicated to himself, and then to the doorway. He offered his other hand, also palm up.

Maria looked at her own hands, palms facing out, and realized the gesture might be giving a mixed message. She shook her head, something only another human would understand. "I really must return to my colleagues, but thank you again," she said, backing away. When she was several steps from the Nyrians she turned and walked as quickly as she could to Nola.

"What was that all about?" she asked when she reached her.

"They wanted to share with you," Nola said.

"Share?"

"Themselves. Their bodies. You. It is their custom," Nola said. "I thought you were going to go! You looked like you were enjoying them."

"Oh my god," Maria said. "This dancing is ..."

"Exciting?"

"That's not the word I was looking for." Maria drew closer to Nola and breathed into her ear. "I want to get you out of here and fuck you senseless!"

"Just me?" Nola asked.

"Just you! As soon as possible," Maria said.

15

Dave spent his alone time bent over his monitor. He watched a live feed from the ship orbiting far above. He split the screen and examined the numbers scrolling across half of the screen. He showed Salia once. The images were strange, of a large empty space inhabited by a glowing machine, yet like no machine she had even seen. She was amazed that she could see something that was so far away. The figures were indecipherable squiggles. He explained that they told him of the health of the reactor. He seemed reassured, so she was pleased. She wanted him to be happy. But the images meant nothing to her. He showed her a feed from the shuttle, the craft he and his crew mates walked out of after it landed on the planet. He pointed at the images: where the pilots sat and controlled the craft, the seats where they all remained as the ship descended, and at the stern of the ship, his all-important reactor.

When city officials, or members of an audience, asked him about the star ship engines, she didn't fail to notice how he tactfully deflected their queries. She was the only Nyrian who saw what was on his device, the only one he shared the secret of the engines with. She didn't understand what she saw—to her it was a mere glowing mechanical machine—but it became their secret, which made her feel closer to him. He described the power the reactors created, the heat of star circulating within their chambers, particles fusing together, molten plasma confined within a magnetic field. She did not follow very much of what he described, but she had the image of a small sun held by strong metal hands and forced to do Dave's bidding. She felt fear at what the humans created, and she felt pride for the man who controlled its amazing power.

When he showed her images of the larger machine, in the great ship orbiting in the sky above with the goddess, she tried to identify another emotion she felt, but could not name it. It was a deep longing, wanting something, but having it withheld. No, it had to do with the reason behind the withholding. There was no word in Nyrian to capture the feeling concisely. Salia knew, in that moment, that Dave cared more about the machine than he did her. And because of that, she didn't like his reactors. They stood between her and the man that filled her. That was okay, she tried to lie to herself. But she didn't really believe it was okay. Regardless, the reactors were important to him. He took his responsibility to them and his captain very seriously.

It wasn't what she wanted or needed. Her needs and wants, she began to accept, were secondary in her relationship with Dave. She resolved herself to accept what she had, which was knowing this wonderful stranger from afar. For so much of her life she felt alien from those around her, as if she were a mutant or freak because she felt a gaping hole that no other felt. And because they did not feel a hole in themselves, no one could fill hers. With the earthling Dave she was given what she so longed for, and despite his preoccupation with machinery, he still touched her emptiness. She cherished that touch.

Salia sat in the adjoining room, with eyes closed, examining herself. She let her awareness hover around the location of her heart. Her mind probed, feeling the tenderness and pain. Her *liaison* was exhausted from the tour. He performed with his colleagues, answering questions about their world. He went to dinners, entertainment, was driven in parades. He vaguely talked about the powerful engines he controlled that moved their ship across space. He described the incredible speeds that were created to move the ship, increasing with each acceleration. Dave spoke of his work as if he were telling a story to youngsters, and maybe that is how he viewed those who questioned him. How could they begin to comprehend what he controlled?

Salia pushed on her chest, trying to imagine the force his engines created when it pushed their ship across the vast expanse. Her hands pressed against her chest, and it comforted her. The quivering around her heart was contained, for a moment, at least. She released the pressure of her hand and began to tap her chest lightly with her finger tips. One two three four five six seven eight, she tapped. She drummed on her chest again, eight times, the hollow thudding calming her. After several minutes, Salia rose and went to the small break room that served the workers on this floor of the building that was offered to the city's guests for the duration of their visit. She found Nola and Cartan sitting at a table and joined them. Nola studied Salia briefly after she sat.

"You look distraught," Nola said.

"I've been away from the crowds too long. I have forgotten how to hide it," Salia answered. "It feels like before."

Nola nodded.

"It has not changed. I am the one that has changed," she added.

Nola turned from her to where she came.

"He seeks solitude. He needs time to recharge," Salia said. "That is what he calls it. He finds the attention overpowering. Even mine, it seems. I know he does not mean to cause pain, but it is a familiar ache." Her colleagues were staring at her, each smiling. Cartan reached out a hand and placed it on Salia's. A tear ran down her cheek.

"I do not understand, but I try. They are a strange people," Salia said.

Salia saw only understanding and love in the other's eyes. They knew her well enough that she needn't explain. But releasing the words lightened a weight within her.

"Where is Maria?" Salia asked.

"She seeks rest," Nola said. "But I think she avoids the others. It is a difficult tour. She told me of her home, how she spends her time when not piloting magnificent star ships. She has a quiet and peaceful life. Her only companion is a creature called Cat."

They didn't notice Dave standing in the doorway. Each jolted with surprise when he laughed. "I'm sorry," he said. "I didn't mean to startle you."

"Have you completed your work?" Salia asked.

"Yes, thank you," Dave answered, sitting next to her and taking her hand. "A cat is perfect for Maria," he said. "They are warm and soft little animals that allow you to stroke them and feed them and are not very demanding, most of the time."

"Like Nola," Salia said.

"I let Maria stroke me, but I am demanding. All of the time," Nola replied.

"We were discussing what curious creatures humans are," Nola added. Salia shot her a glance, but Dave only laughed again.

"You don't know the half of it," Dave said.

"You must find Nyrians equally perplexing," Nola said.

"Well, I thought I was getting somewhere, but then we ... met the others."

"There is a story," Nola said, "about the creation of Nyria and its people. Would you like to hear it?" she asked.

"Please," Dave answered.

"There are many creation stories, and this is just was one of them. It is just a story. When we are children, we believe it is the truth. And maybe it is. But as we mature, we understand stories differently. This story begins before history and memory, as creation stories must. They all begin with 'in the beginning' and this story is no different. In the beginning, there were three types of Nyrians. There were male and female, as we see. However, there was a third type of Nyrian, round in form. This type had four arms, and four legs, and two heads and two sexual organs, one male and one female. Or sometimes they had both male, or both female parts. These round Nyrians were very powerful. Imagine! They had twice the strength, and twice the intelligence, of the other Nyrians."

Nola stopped to make sure the others were listening. They were.

"The goddess, protecting us from above, round and powerful, created these special beings. But she was not the only goddess. Nyrians have many goddesses and gods to protect them. There is the distant sun lighting the sky, in thrall to the goddess, even letting himself be consumed by her, for a time."

"*Heimal*," Dave interrupted.

"Yes, exactly," Nola said. "But there is also the god Cila, circling the great mother, competing with Nyria for her attention. And the dancing lights that fill the darkened sky during *Heimal*. You will see them soon, Dave. Each type of Nyrian sprung from one of these different gods. The solitary male were offspring of the sun. The sun is alone in the sky and needs no other. It radiates its own power and shares it.

The solitary female came from Cila, though some say that they were created by the dancing lights. They equally offer their light, without inhibition or qualification. They do not understand concepts such as loneliness or need. Their needs are mutual, and mutually shared, with each other.

"But the complete beings, the powerful ones, were birthed by the great mother, the goddess above," Nola continued. "As I said, these original beings were stronger than the others. Twice as strong! But their strength bred hubris. It is a good word to describe them, and the feelings they must have had towards the others. Their pride and confidence made them look down on the others. Whatever it was they did or wanted, it angered the other gods. These gods felt threatened by the powerful and complete beings. And not just the gods—the others, too. They also felt threatened and resentful of the strength of the complete beings. So, when the goddess was sleeping during the long night when the stars dance in the sky and Cila can be seen as a bright light, the gods acted, even the hidden sun, and cut the complete Nyrians in half.

"After they did so, they forced the once whole beings to see their wound before the gods healed it, forcing them to see their defeat and remember their loss and pain. They were not satisfied with separating and weakening these beings, they wanted them to always live with the pain of separation. As their original form was cut and removed, they found themselves able to live, but always longing for their other side! One half was a woman, and the other half was a man, or the halves were both man, or both woman. Whatever the original arrangement, they longed for their other half. It was a longing that shaped their very existence, and they spent their lives searching for their matching half, so that they could be whole once again."

"That is not just a story," Salia whispered.

"I know," Nola agreed. "It is our story. I told Maria this. I told her we must have been two females bound together before we were split. But she insisted the story was metaphor. A description of love. She said that when opposite sides meet, they experience the wonder of love. This love is stronger than any other thing, even joining," Nola said smiling. "Love is the joy and connection beyond the act of touch and penetration. Joining itself can be mere metaphor, allowing for the briefest of time the physical wholeness that was denied when we were torn apart. It allows us to be welded together, to be healed and whole again, if only for a moment."

"The others," Dave asked, "the ones that were not split ..."

"You have met them," Nola said. "You are among them. I could ask you your thoughts."

Dave started to laugh, but stopped it when it was only a breath and a smile. "They don't seem to ..."

"Yearn for another," Salia finished.

"Maybe it is just metaphor, like every story, but it's a good one," Dave said. "It's lonely being alive, so we seek our better half. Our soulmate."

"All humans are lonely?" Nola asked.

"Every single one of them," Dave said. "The entire planet. And if they told you otherwise, they'd be lying. I'm sure you've seen that already. We don't hide it very well."

"That is hard for me to believe. A planet of lonely, yearning beings?" Nola asked.

Dave looked at the woman opposite and nodded. "We spend a lifetime searching," he said, glancing down at his hands so he would not be tempted to look at Salia, whom he was actually speaking to. "Sometimes we find it, and we're lucky and keep it. Sometimes we let it go, because we're scared, or we're lazy and don't want to put in the work. Sometimes we make up excuses, about it happening too fast or too soon, and ... sometimes, if I'm honest, we don't think we're worthy of it. Humans tend to have weak images of themselves. Or we're just plain stupid, and walk away or wreck what we could have had."

And which one are you? He expected one of them to ask, but they didn't. They were too understanding and kind to do that. *Which one am I?* he asked himself instead. He raised his eyes and smiled at Salia, realizing that he did love her, and because of that, he didn't want to hurt her. But he was going to anyway.

He tried to lighten the silence, and his own mood. "This is all top secret, though," he joked, "not to be shared off planet earth." But nobody laughed.

"It sounds so beautiful," Cartan said.

"Which part?" Dave asked.

"Searching. Finding. Losing. Growing. An entire planet of beings united in their loneliness."

Dave let Cartan's words slowly sink before replying. "*United in their loneliness,*" he repeated. "It doesn't feel like that. It can also be painful."

"Same-same," Cartan observed.

"Yeah," Dave nodded. "I get it. Same-same."

16

The airship approached across fields of ripened crops, buffeted by strong winds that blew down from the hills. In the long spring of Nyria, the years and months between *Heimal*, clouds from the great ocean paused at the range, dropping their rain and water the fields that grew in a continuous cycle of tending and harvesting and planting. The fertile lands made the city of Alram prosperous, and because of its prosperity, many came to play a part in its success. There was a role for any that came.

Earlier in her life, Ceera had passed through the city. She didn't know while she struggled to fit in that the man who would play a significant part in helping her find a place in the world was actually in the city at the same time. Tauma taught at the university. She never crossed his path while she was there studying wireless communications. Tauma spoke little about his time there, but the institution wished to host their now famous alumni and his alien guests, so he accepted. In a collective those who can advance the common good are celebrated. The invitation was one that was expected, and that could not be declined.

The secondary airfield was visible ahead, their initial landing site abandoned because of autumn winds. The ship descended, trying to avoid the worst of the unpredictable gusts, aiming for the tethering polls and the waiting ground crew. Alan reached for a seatbelt that he knew wasn't there, gave up the search, and took Ceera's hand instead. It was their sixth city. Speeches, dinners, entertainment. Questions. Alan looked at his crewmates and knew the exhaustion was not only his. On earth he felt like a celebrity, a returning hero. Here, he felt … Ceera could not comprehend the concept of a zoo, or why an animal would be kept, but she understood his wish to end the parade. Her reasons were partly selfish—she wanted to savor this man herself and not share him at all. Their time together was a commodity she wished to hoard, and at every place they went it was taken from her. Every engagement was another reminder of the future separation that haunted them.

The ship lurched as it was tied down, fighting vainly to fly away with the winds, but it was soon secured and winched safety to the ground. They disembarked and made their way quickly down the gangplank, shivering, before entering the vehicles waiting to whisk them into the city. As soon as the doors closed, it silently rolled away. Thanh explained the technology weeks prior, excited about its elegant simplicity, critical of its weaknesses, and praising its cleanliness. Creating power from the heat beneath their feet, funneling that power into light and energy dense lithium-sulfur batteries. Because of the power steaming up through the planetary crust, the Nyrians seemed to leapfrog earth's self-destructive infatuation with carbon-based fuels. Alan forgot most of his colleague's words. At first, he was annoyed by the smell in each of the cities they visited that reminded him of rotten eggs, but now he hardly noticed.

The university Rector stood on the stairs at the grand entrance of the administration block to welcome the strange beings. He strode down the steps as their transports stopped and bowed as they gathered before him.

"Welcome," he said. "It is an honor to have you grace our institution with your presence." He directed his words at the woman who led the visitors.

"Thank you for inviting us," Inessa replied.

The Rector smiled as her words were translated in a device created on campus from a printer replicated from the human's device. The power source of the human's machine would require more study, but he was pleased at the technical departments ingenuity in finding a local solution.

"Professor Tauma," he said, bowing to Inessa's companion. "I am humbled by your return. Your brilliance was not fully appreciated during your tenure here. Regardless, the results of your experiment prove any doubters were mistaken."

Tauma tilted his head in a slight bow. "Professor Sana," he replied.

Inessa didn't need a translator to interpret the tension between the two. Tauma told her of the humiliation and ridicule he was subjected to when he proposed messaging the stars, including from their distinguished host. He was not only a solitary, tolerated because his research did not require others, but his findings showed he was obviously crazed as well.

"Such a lovely place of study," Inessa cut in. "Professor Tauma has told us that we will be amazed with the facilities."

He turned his full attention to her, dismissing his former colleague. "Indeed, you will," he answered. "If you are amenable, I can begin the tour now."

"That would be wonderful, Professor Sana," she replied.

"As the morning has brought a warning frost let us begin inside," he said. "I have a wonderful surprise in the technical department. Please follow me."

"I was enraptured by the devices you sent into our atmosphere," Sana said once they entered a technical department's laboratory. "And how Probe Controller Gunther de Haas commanded them from your ship orbiting so far away. Superb work."

"Thank you," Gunther said.

"And far beyond our technological ability," Sana said. "But we Nyrians crawl forward, and thanks to your example, slowly advance. It appears that I, despite leading a great learning institution, am but a student."

He waited. The humans didn't know what for. "So, by utilizing Professor Tauma's enhanced radio transmission," he continued, "and by incorporating the device-to-device communication capability of your translating buds—a wonderful device, I must say, not only its ability to break down barriers, but communicating without the need of a transmitting station. Amazing—So, utilizing your example, we have made a step. Watch," he said, and pointed to a far door that stood open.

A technician entered with a box and stood next to Sana. The Rector nodded and the technician operated a joy stick protruding from the box. Whirling sounds came from the doorway, and a miniature airship flew into the room. It circled the group, hovered above them, and descended slowly. Instead of a gondola, a tray of drinks hung suspended beneath.

"It is called *raina*, a delicious warmed drink to be enjoyed on chilly mornings like this one," Sana announced. "Please, take a cup."

After they approached and took a glass, the little airship rose, circled the room once again, and flew through the door. The technician followed behind.

"A remotely controlled airship," Sana pronounced proudly. "Nothing like the probes you controlled from afar. I would very much like to learn more from you during your visit to this center of learning."

The party stood silent after he spoke, glancing from their drinks to each other.

Sana sensed their discomfort and tried to shoo it away. "As I said, it is an honor to have you here," he said. "Let us walk, see the university, and get to know each other better."

"Thank you, Professor Sana," Inessa said graciously. "That would be wonderful."

His mind is a hungry beast, Tauma warned Inessa. *He hears everything and he forgets nothing. And he takes what he learns and turns it to his advantage. He copies, and he improves. His drive knows no limit, if he believes it will improve society. He seemed to know everything about my work, well before I lectured about it. And he pretended to support me just long enough to let me finish. Then he saw that I was disrobed as a threat to the learning collective.*

"You seemed quite engaged with the Rector," Inessa said to Thanh. "What did you discuss?"

"He was very interested in the concept of competition," Thanh answered.

"Competition?"

"It doesn't exist as such in Nyrian society. Everybody finds a role a performs it. I don't even know how we got on the subject," he said.

"Think about it," Inessa told him. She quizzed each of her crew on their interactions with the Rector, trying to gleam how much information he might have on earth and its capabilities.

"I don't know," Thanh admitted. "He asked about our skin, why it was different shades, so I told him about plate tectonics—which he already knew about, because I've talked about it in our visits. They don't have tectonics here. It's just one supercontinent with lots of hotspots underneath. Utterly fascinating."

"Plate tectonics," Inessa repeated.

"That's right. That's okay, isn't it?"

"Yes, of course," Inessa said, "it's a perfectly benign subject."

"He was curious about … how humans looking different, speaking different languages and living great distances apart 'shared knowledge', as he put it. I laughed a little at that, and he asked me what was funny. I think I said that we didn't always share so nicely. I tried to go back to geography, but he was very interested in what I meant. I think I said that sometimes some people were forced to share if they weren't keen to do so. If force were used, what kind of force, he wanted to know. He didn't want to let it go. I'm sorry, Inessa," Thanh said.

"What did you tell him? About trade and colonialism?"

"Oh, God no," Thanh said. "I told him about people trading with each other, exchanging goods that the other might not have. Then I told him how being distant caused each people to try to keep up with the other, how seeing another place make an advancement forced others to advance. He was very interested in that. He said that it sounded very inefficient."

"You were talking about aircraft?" Inessa whispered the words, but couldn't hide the reprimand within them.

"He brought it up," Maria said. "He even reminded me when I mentioned it. He knows everything we've said on this tour. In the first city we visited, a Nyrian asked that if lands on earth were separated by oceans, how did we travel around. It just slipped out."

"I remember," Inessa said.

"Sana was, I don't know, *intrigued* by the concept of heavier than air machines flying great distances," Maria said. "I mean, he can already see it, with the shuttle we landed in."

"Is that all?"

"No, I think he was more interested in the kind of power it takes to keep something so heavy aloft. He started talking about liquids that burned, and elements that—"

"Send in Dave, please," Inessa said.

"Would you like to see our Geothermal Enhancement Department, Reactor Technician Dave Wise?" Sana asked. The human would no doubt tell him to use a single name, but at their level of expertise, the university Rector found the custom not only odd and belittling, but uncomfortable.

"Please, call me Dave," the human replied. He found himself alone with the Nyrian, failing to notice when the others were led into another department.

"Surely, on Earth, you must be referred to as Professor, at least?" Sana asked.

"No," the human said, making a short barking sound. "Doctor, sometimes. It's the name of a degree, the highest in a field. And the last name. Doctor Wise. But mostly it's first name. I am sure it is just cultural. Where Gunther is from, I believe they value titles."

"I will remember that," Sana said. "If you will permit me, may I call you Doctor Wise? Perhaps it is just my culture. Your work and expertise demand more than a single name."

"Sure," Dave agreed.

"Do you know what the biggest problem with Nyrians is, Doctor Wise?"

Dave continued to follow Sana. They walked up well-worn steps and through large doors made of glass and entered a wide room. The sound of their shoes squeaking on polished tiles filled the empty place.

Dave shook his head. When Sana didn't react to the gesture, Dave added the word: "No."

"They are content," Sana said. "They all fit in. They all have a role. They have no needs, as all their needs are met. They have no wants, because everything is theirs. Have you not found this so?" he asked.

"Well—"

"And as result," Sana carried on, "they have no ambition. That is left to the likes of myself, and the universities. We here continually work to better the whole. But what I gather from yourself and your distinguished colleagues is that that is not the case on earth. Sometimes you create new and magnificent inventions, simply because you can. Although you do not seem to like to talk about that, if I not mistaken."

"No—"

"But such creations your species have made!" Sana continued. "Astrogator Chen Li has told me that humans looked up into their night sky, saw the many distant stars, and were so driven to learn more that they created the means to visit them. That is ambition!"

"I think—"

"The energy required to escape the planet's gravitational pull must have created such an obstacle," Sana mused. "Gravity is a hand that pulls everything from the sky, even airships. And yet your vessels slip so easily through its grasp. That kind of power is a wonderful achievement. Don't you consider it as such?"

Dave waited for Sana to continue talking, but the silence told him the Rector actually wanted to hear what he had to say.

"Yes, indeed," Dave admitted. "One of humanity's greatest. But it didn't come without a cost."

"A cost?" Sana asked. "Are you willing to elaborate."

"Finding a power source that does not pollute the atmosphere, like carbon-based fuels, or kill everything near it with radiation should something go wrong, even when it goes right," Dave said. "It took generations to find a clean energy source. You have avoided much of what we did not, harnessing the heat beneath your feet. You are very fortunate. Is this where you study geothermal dynamics?" he said, trying to wrest control of the conversation and its direction.

"Yes, we are fortunate, our needs are met, but we lack ambition," Sana said, ignoring Dave's question. "I must bow before your achievements. Unlimited power to advance your civilization, to make distance, and time, insignificant."

Inessa put a finger to her mouth as they entered their accommodation floor. She looked inside the lamps, quietly opened drawers, examined bed frames. Eva realized what she was doing and helped search. The Nyrians stood and watched as other crew silently joined Inessa and Eva. Ariana stopped and waved her arms to catch the others attention. She showed them a small device hidden behind a headboard. Jardin located another in an overhead light. Abede removed one from behind a small cupboard beside his bed.

"They're jammed now," Eva said, typing onto her wrist pad. "It's basic technology, mid twentieth century, at least."

"Still effective," Inessa said. "If we didn't suspect anything. Son of a bitch."

"He knows your technology is far more advanced than ours," Tauma said. "He wants to learn. It is his job."

"You sound like you're excusing him," Inessa replied.

"Certainly not," Tauma said. "I know Rector Sana too well for that. He will have hung on every word any of you have uttered since arriving. Any description of earth, any mention of technology—"

"Why doesn't he just come out and ask? Instead, he bugs our accommodation," Inessa said.

"If he asked, you wouldn't tell him," Tauma said. "That is a fact. You told me yourself. It devours Sana that there are things he does not understand. You are a treasure trove of secrets he cannot have. I have underestimated what may he do to get them."

Inessa walked towards the doorway. "Don't bother unpacking," she said. "We won't be staying long." Reaching out her palm she added, "Give me the bugs."

Ariana, Jardin, and Abede stepped forward and deposited the devices into her hand. Tauma walked to her and placed his hand over hers.

"Let me return these to him," he asked. "I am your *liaison*. It is proper," he added softly when she failed to hand them over. She nodded and released her grip, depositing them into his open palm.

"Gather by the entrance and we will make our way to the airship," he said. "It is time to go home, before the weather changes."

Inessa kissed his cheek and he strode out of the room. Turning to tell her crew and their Nyrian liaisons to ready to leave, she saw they were all waiting, bags in hand. She led them through the corridor leading to the building's grand entrance. Down an adjoining corridor they heard loud voices, their translators catching a word or two in a stream of noise, struggling to find an earth-based equivalent.

"... impinged the *integrity*"

"... *traitor* to your people"

"... irrevocably damage the *reputation*"

"... never be *secure* again ..."

With translators turned off, the humans would have heard something similar to the screech of angry eagles. With them on, they could only tell who was speaking from the context of their words—one criticizing the other's action, the other issuing naked threats. Alan glanced at Ceera who stood wide eyed, listening. Finally, Tauma marched alone down the corridor, went to the entrance door and opened it. He breathed heavily, but spoke calmly.

"If you will," he said, motioning outside. "Transport will arrive shortly."

By the time the party reached the last step, two transports arrived. They climbed aboard and were whisked to the airfield outside the city where the airship strained against its tethers, trying to break free in the increasing winds. They quickly ascended the gangplank, and as they reached their seats, the ship leapt from its restraints and sped away in the cold currents of air.

"He didn't want you to leave," Tauma said, his first words since leaving the university. "He looked forward to entertaining you for the duration of *Heimal*. He would have made sure you were comfortable, and unable to refuse, as soon the weather will not permit travel."

"Are you okay?" Inessa asked.

"During the dark time, all will be okay," he answered, "*Heimal* is a time for inward looking. The cities do not trade, and the airships do not fly. In the Institute, it is a time for research and reflection." But he knew Sana would think of little more than what mysteries the humans were withholding. It would devour the man, Tauma thought with satisfaction.

17

Alan woke to find the dented pillow and crumpled sheets beside him empty. He peered into the small kitchen and smiled, watching as Ceera made the hot black drink he liked in the morning. She found the smell more appealing than the bitter taste, but shared in the ritual, sipping a small part of his home world with him. She knew he was watching as she prepared the brew. She wore only his crew sweatshirt and nothing else. It excited him when she wore it that way. When they finished the drink, they would make love. Another morning ritual. She poured the hot drinks into ceramic cups and brought them to the bed, where he waited, a small mound in the covers giving away his anticipation.

She sat cross legged in front of him, and scrunched her nose as she sipped. Alan inhaled the aroma with eyes closed, then slowly touched the cup to his lips and took some of the liquid into his mouth. When he opened his eyes, he saw her smiling at him.

"Good morning," he said.

"Good morning," she replied.

"You're up early," he said, looking at the gloom out the window.

"No, I am not," she said. "You are up late. I gave up waiting so I made noise in the kitchen."

"Then why is it so ... why is it not very light outside?" he asked.

"It is beginning," Ceera answered. "We have much to do today, so enjoy your kahffee. Straight to work as soon as you finish."

"Straight to work?"

"Straight. No time to waste. Up and at it," she said.

"Straight to work?" he asked again, closing one eye in a gesture she now understood.

"Maybe not straight. Maybe flat, maybe sitting. Maybe from behind," she answered. "Then straight to work."

Alan took another drink, held his cup with one hand and let the other glide along Ceera's thigh.

"Inessa's broadcast last night was very beautiful," she said, ignoring his hand. "She showed a deep understanding of what *Heimal* means. And she was very gracious to Rector Sana."

"That's called politics," Alan said.

Ceera took another small sip of the black drink and waited.

"She is placating him, stroking his ego, if he has something like that, and letting him think he might get what he wants when the goddess returns," Alan said. "She's letting him know he went too far, but is keeping it between them. He knows what she meant when she used certain words."

"And blah, blah, blah," Ceera said. "Are you finished with you kahffee? Will you *join* with me now?"

Alan gulped what remained in his cup, took hers and finished its contents, and set both on the bedside table before unfolding her legs so she could climb onto his waiting lap.

Ceera stacked the vehicle batteries in the rear compartment while Alan stowed food, bedding and clothing. Most of the clothing was borrowed from the Nyrians. The crew of the *Sunspot* travelled light, and the only season prepared for was the controlled environment of their ship. Aside from flight suit, track suit top and bottoms, and a light dress uniform expected to be worn twice (on reaching orbit around the target planet and on return to earth), the humans were not prepared for any type of weather. Alan shivered, despite wearing two pairs of socks and a coat made of a wool like fabric manufactured from the bark of trees.

"You don't look prepared for winter," Inessa said as she watched him stuff gear into the small transport.

"I'm not," he admitted. "But Ceera says we'll be fine. Lots of gear already at the cabin."

"Then I'm sure you'll be fine," Inessa said. "But I want daily check-ins anyway. If you go silent, we'll have to go looking for you. And maintain your watch schedule. Contact me if anything needs review. No hesitation."

"Understood," Alan answered.

"I don't like separating the team," she said, "but ... have a good time."

"Thank you," Alan replied.

"Just don't forget the check-ins."

Ceera drove over the saddle, leaving the small settlement of the transmitting station behind. Alan gazed at the distant mountains, their summits painted with a dusting of snow. The gas giant above was a deep purple as shadow slowly overtook it. Ceera stopped the vehicle and they watched the faraway light of Cila shown against her mother's darkening face. Then the light of the moon faded out as the eclipse plunged it into its own long darkness. Ceera drove on, the narrow road becoming lightly covered in snow the higher they climbed. She turned on lights to help illuminate their way forward.

After three hours they neared the cabin and Ceera guided the vehicle to a stop beside the small structure. Just as Ceera described, the cabin sat beside a small lake, and was surrounded by the rocky terrain that sloped up, forming a secluded bowl. A thin glassy surface already began to spread along the edges of the water. Soon it would join in the middle and become thick enough to cross.

"Come," Ceera said, opening her door and letting frigid air in.

Alan shivered before jumping out and following her. She led the way to a front porch overlooking the water and opened the door of the cabin. Alan expected cold, dark and dusty, cobwebs in corners (despite not seeing any spiders on Nyria), and mouse droppings on counter tops. What he found was quite different. Ceera activated lights and the room lit up. She took off her coat and Alan realized he wasn't cold at all. He copied her as she slipped out of her shoes and socks and felt the warmth of the floor through the soles of his feet. She kept stripping off clothing and Alan kept pace, until they stood naked, facing each other.

"Welcome home," she said, stepping close to him.

He welcomed her body, wrapping her in his arms.

"Let me show you around," she said.

"I think I get the lay out," he said, breathing in the scent of her hair. Over her shoulder he saw a kitchenette, a lounge with sofa and chair, a squat iron box he hoped was a wood burning stove, and a very inviting bed nestled in the corner. He lifted her and carried her towards it. She reached down and pulled back the bedding and he lay her on the soft mattress. She pulled him on top of her, guiding him in and shared his energy leisurely as the world outside darkened.

After, and before he could drift to sleep, Ceera shook Alan. "Come my love," she said. "We must go outside."

He moaned contently, reached for her, but she was already up and dressing. He joined her, putting layers back on, and she grabbed a blanket from the bed and pulled him towards the door by his hand. Cold air filled his lungs as they stepped outside. Ceera draped the blanket around their shoulders and sat with him on the edge of the porch. She pointed to the sky and Alan could just make out a faint light. He watched it longer and it grew in brightness. Ceera pointed in another direction and at another faint light.

"The night begins," she said.

"Stars!"

"Soon there will be many. So many."

Alan shifted closer to, cocooned in their blanket they watched stars appear. As the cold night deepened and a chill crept in, she got to her feet.

"Now we unload," she announced, "and then we go back to bed."

Alan woke in the dark, not knowing what time it was. He heard Ceera breathe softly next to him. He slipped out of bed and into his track suit. Stepping quietly across the heated floor, he felt his way to the kitchenette before turning on and dimming a light. The windows outside were opaque, as if painted black. All he could see was his own reflection. He checked the time and confirmed that it was late morning. Sliding a finger over his tablet, he keyed in a brief message to keep Inessa happy. *All okay. Warm and cozy.*

He set up a coffee and placed it on the hot pad. He adjusted the heat to high and thermal steam raced up a pipe beneath the cabin and into the small coil beneath the percolator. Tauma built the cabin well, insulated thoroughly and warmed by tapping into the heat beneath the mountains. It was designed for *Heimal*, and he used it for his retreat before the first of his small group began to show up at the station far below. As the group grew, he shared it with them, and the cabin held a special meaning to each.

The heat pad soon glowed red. The sound of the coffee maker might wake Ceera, but what better way to wake in the morning? Scratch that, he thought, smiling at the woman sleeping in the nearby bed. There were better ways. The sound and smell of coffee was just a good one. Alan tried to peer out the window and only watched his reflected face grow closer. On the windowsill was a small collection of polished and shaped stones, placed carefully in a line. He picked one up. It looked like a misshapen bird egg and fit into the center of his palm as if made to sit there.

Alan set the stone back in its place on the ledge as the coffee began to percolate. He removed the pot from the heat and it grew quiet. Turning to see if it disturbed Ceera, he saw her leaning on an elbow, watching him and smiling. He poured two cups of coffee and returned to bed. Ceera took one, smelled the rich aroma, and placed it on the small table beside the bed. Alan sat against the headboard and sipped.

"I see you found my secrets," she said.

"Your what?" he asked.

In answer, she got out of bed and padded naked to the kitchen window. She picked up the stone Alan had examined and returned to bed with it. She sat next to him and held the stone in her hand, turning and studying it.

"They are all my secrets," she said. "This one I found beside a large tree outside Turun. You haven't been to Turun yet. It is not a very pretty city, and I didn't stay long. It was becoming very uncomfortable, and at every accommodation I stayed there were those who wanted to share, and who didn't understand not sharing."

"Why are you ... different?" he asked.

"I don't know," she said. "I felt like a freak until I met Tauma. He really saved me. When I first stayed with him, I waited for hours, expecting him to want me to share, laying in his guest bed with the covers pulled to my chin. But he never came in. I must have looked tired in the morning, because he asked about my sleep. And being tired I told him the truth. I thought he would cast me out, but he just sat down opposite and said that as long as I stayed with him, I would only share what I wanted, and was willing, to share, and with whom I chose."

"Sounds normal," Alan said.

"It is not normal," Ceera responded. "But he said it as if it was natural, and with him it was. As it was with Cartan, and Daan, and Hylva, and the others you know."

"But in the cities ..."

"You've seen them," Ceera said. "*They* are natural and normal. Not me. So, I moved a lot. But Turun is not a big place, no crowds to disappear in, and I left. But as I did, I stopped beside a large tree. It moved its branches as I came close, but I felt like it was doing more. Like it was pointing. Trees do not point, I know. But I looked, and below the tips of the leaves was this stone."

She held the stone in her fingers and lifted it. "I carried it with me all the way to the transport station, and held it during the entire journey, before I put it in my bag with my other secrets. When I first came here, I knew this was where they wanted to be, so I placed them below the window, where they can see the world outside from a safe and welcome place."

She held out the stone and Alan set down his coffee and took it. He turned it reverently and examined it again, before nestling it in his palm.

"Why is it a secret?" he asked.

"You've met the others," Ceera said, smiling softly. "Nyrians don't have possessions, not even their bodies. Everything belongs to all, so there is no me or mine. If there is a tool not being used, then it is free to be used. If there is a body alone, then it can be shared. It is the way of things. But my secrets belong only to me. I didn't share them. I held them close, away from any other, hidden. Like me, hidden deep inside while others used what they wanted. My secrets brought comfort, during many times when it would have been easier to exit."

Alan heard a slight catch in her voice but remained silent beside her. "Many choose to exit," Ceera said. "But my secrets kept me here, and led me to you."

She looked at him with moist eyes, reached out and closed his hand around the stone. "And this one is now yours," she said. "My secret for you to keep."

"I'll cherish it forever," he said, wrapping his arms around her, where they stayed as the coffee grew cold and the dark outside continued.

Clouds formed over the great ocean of Nyria and drifted over the land. Newly revealed stars became faint, and then unseen, behind a dark blanket. In the mountains snowflakes began to silently fall, covering all in white. Then, as the planet cooled, the snow fell across the great plains, along the rivers, the deltas, and even at the coast. The darkened goddess slumbered as her devoted daughter was cloaked in a white gown. Alan and Ceera, inside their warm cocoon, didn't notice the change until they opened their door and were subsumed by silence. They stood together, staring into the darkness, as ghostly flakes fell outside. Gone were the surrounding peaks, gone the lake, gone the path. All was concealed. They retreated into their refuge, and still the snow fell. After two weeks, as if the world were gasping for breath, the skies finally cleared.

Ceera took a blanket from the bed, draped it around her shoulders, and led Alan outside. Once on the porch, she invited him to share the covering and gazed upward into the black expanse. Thousands upon thousands of stars shimmered in the frigid sky, forming a familiar arch, a view into their shared galactic home. Alan looked for familiar features—Orion the warrior, sword at his belt, Ursa Major, the great bear, Sagittarius, the nighttime scorpion—but couldn't see them. The heavens were a mystery, the vista too distant to be recognizable.

Ceera told her own stories about the designs in the Nyrian sky. Pointing, she indicated Albra, leading her carriage. And the great seabird, Phonece. And Jara, the god of fire who dwells below, but is mirrored in the darkest sky. Alan tried to follow her finger, searching for the bright stars with strange names and the shapes her ancestors saw high above them. He could only see the many pinpricks of light filling the night sky. He gazed at the disc of the Milky Way splashed across the scene and examined the edge, where the star his home planet circled may have been, but it was too dim to be seen even on such a clear night. Alan moved his hand over a random area, because he had no real idea, when Ceera asked from where he came. They both stood and contemplated the area, searching out each other's hand beneath the blanket.

"Let's go for a walk," Ceera suggested, returning to the warmth of the cabin and selecting more clothes.

Once fortified with more layers she pulled equipment out of the storage cupboard and handed Alan two smooth, armlength planks. Growing up near the mountains, he had owned snowshoes, as well as Nordic skis and snowboards. What Ceera handed him looked like those had all had a child together. She laughed as he turned them over and examined them, searching for a way in. Sitting him down on the porch, she guided each foot into the proper place and tightened them before doing her own. She stepped off and onto the new snow, her shoes keeping her from sinking. She moved one foot forward and glided, then moved the other, and was quickly ten meters from Alan.

He stepped onto the snow and felt himself sink, so he shifted his weight and stepped with the other foot. His ankle pivoted and he glided smoothly across the powder. As he passed Ceera, she moved forward, stepping with him and keeping pace, and they descended the hidden bank and continued over the lake. Starlight illuminated the scene before them. Ceera grabbed Alan's arm and they stopped. He pulled her close, and they stood beneath a dome of stars. She gripped tighter and gasped as the first lights flickered. Alan gazed at the spectacle, unsure if he were seeing meteorites, frozen crystals in the atmosphere, or some form of life living high above. They both stood mutely, necks tilted back, mouths slightly open and watched the lights dance above.

18

Dave slid his finger over his tablet, moving the view through the vast reactor of the *Sunspot*. He examined the blue glow of the centrifuge, which kept the plasma within circulating and at extreme temperature. It could stay in that state of perpetual readiness for a hundred years or more. He reviewed feeds from other departments, analyzing energy transfers and power flows. Content with what he saw, he passed his hand over the tablet and pulled up the feed from the shuttle. He increased the temperature of the reactor and vented excess heat. The snow building up around the base of the ship quickly melted. He scrolled through motion activated and heat sensitive cameras placed around the hamlet, a habit that became part his shutting down routine. Each feed showed an undisturbed blanket of snow.

He put the tablet away in its case and watched Salia cooking in the kitchen. It was her way of giving him space in the small house. She moved carefully, making little noises she wasn't aware she made. He got up and went to her, kissing the nape of her neck before tasting the food she prepared.

"So good," he said.

"Save it for the others," she chided.

She left the kitchen and put on her coat and set out her snow boots before returning to collect the dish. Dave joined her at the door, suitably dressed for the cold outside. He slid his tablet into his pocket, and they walked over the packed snow to the settlement's commonroom. Others were already there, and placed their offering in the middle of the wide table. Shortly after the snows came, they came together in an unusual celebration the humans explained was called 'Christmas', where they gave each other items that then belonged solely to the receiver of the gift. Dave utilized the station's work shop to craft Salia a smooth metal band to adorn her hand, which he slipped onto a finger. Salia had not taken it off since he placed it there, nor did she ever intend on to do so.

Seeing Dave make the effort to be social warmed her deeply. She knew the effort was for her. He suggested a holiday from his home called a 'thanksgiving,' and it was this they celebrated with shared food. As the weeks passed, the couple found a balance that made both of them happy. Dave had time for himself, she shared her life and herself with him, and they became part of an extended family. For the first time in her life, Salia admitted that she not only felt happy, but complete.

In the common room, Salia set their dish beside the others on the long table. She saw Gunther's cinnamon swirls and her stomach growled, anticipating her favorite dessert. When the table was laden with food and everybody was sitting, the room grew quiet and they looked at Dave. Salia nudged him under the table and he cleared his throat.

"Once again it is a pleasure to be together," he began. "Though the days are dark and cold, it is warm here with you. Every year my family would gather, to spend time, to eat, to reconnect. I had a big family, so tonight, looking at this full table, I feel truly thankful we are together." He smiled at Salia, and then at the others. "Before we would eat, my father always said a blessing, but he isn't with us, so I guess that is for me to do now."

He took Salia's hand in his left and Ariana's in his right. They took the hand next to them until the circle was complete. "We thanked our god for his bounty, but I've learned there are many gods. Or maybe they are all the same, in some way. So, I will offer thanks to that essence behind it all, or in it all, in all of us, for the opportunity to be here, right now, and share *sustenance,* and to celebrate our *union.*"

He saw heads nod around the table. "So, let's eat," he said. *Because the game will be on soon*, the memory of his father added. Platters full of food passed around the table. He picked up his glass of herbal infused water, clinked it against Salia's, and swallowed a mouthful.

"Your countryman, Alan, would appreciate this night, no?" Jardin said. "An American tradition."

Dave turned to his right and raised his glass to the Argentine sitting next to him. "He would, I think," Dave admitted. He examined his glass. "Though I'm sure he'd point out we're drinking water rather wine. And that there is no turkey. Or cranberry sauce. Or pumpkin pie."

"Pumpkin pie," Jardin said. "I never understood the concept."

"It is a wonderful concept," Dave said, "especially with whipped cream on top."

"Do you understand what this man is saying?" Jardin asked Salia.

"I hear his words, but I do not know what they mean," she said.

"That makes two of us," he replied.

"When it rains hard, he tells me small animals are falling from the sky," she said. Jardin laughed. "And when he is impatient waiting for me, he tells me to shake my body."

"Shake a leg," Dave corrected.

"Exactly. I understand his words, but I do not understand what he is saying." She put a hand on Dave's leg under the table. "Even with this bud in my ear, he still speaks an alien language."

They grew quiet when they noticed the others had stopped talking. They followed their eyes to Inessa, who intently examined her wrist pad. She glanced at the door and then returned to her pad. Dave rose and went to his coat, withdrew his tablet and studied it. Motion detectors flashed in the screen. He pulled one up and saw dark images move past the camera. He pulled up another and the shape of a vehicle passed by, the prints of its ski tracks left in the snow. He turned to the shuttle and saw the unmistakable outline of men standing below it.

"There are intruders in the compound," Inessa said.

"Are you sure?" Tauma asked.

"No doubt," she said, showing him her wrist pad, switching from camera to camera. Tracks in snow near the perimeter, figures moving near the shuttle, clearer images of men in the compound. They watched the screen as two kicked in the door to Tauma's house and entered. On another screen a group of eight neared the common room. She zoomed in on the images and saw the cylindrical weapons they carried in their gloved hands.

"Dave, secure the reactor and the shuttle," she ordered, "activate extreme protocol execution, should that be necessary. The rest of—assume we are in a hostile environment. Passive resistance only. Do not respond with violence."

The crew locked their devices, and powered them down. They took them off the wrists and placed the now useless objects on the table in front of them.

"Do you know who they are?" she asked Tauma.

"Sana is behind this," Tauma answered.

Dave sent an alert to the only human not present, and with a swipe of finger transferred control of the *Sunspot* and the shuttle systems to Alan when the door to the common room burst in. Eight Nyrians surrounded the table. Inessa pressed an alert on her wrist pad, another shout to Alan, as well as a warning for the computer running the internal systems on the *Sunspot*. She then made the device inert, took it off and tossed it on the table where it landed next to her half-eaten meal.

Dave continued working on his tablet, sending instructions to Alan. As a Nyrian approached, Dave dropped his pad on the floor and smashed it with his heal, and it cracked. His world went white with pain as a Nyrian hit him in the head with the butt of his weapon. Salia rose from her chair, stepped away as one of the intruders grabbed for her, and bent over Dave. She touched his head gently, pulling back her hand with blood on it. Salia helped him to his feet and glared at the man with the weapon. The Nyrian raised his weapon and struck Dave in the chest. He staggered back, gasping. Salia turned, her face set, and stepped between the man and Dave. The Nyrian slapped her across face.

"Enough of this foolishness!" a voice boomed, and they turned to see Sana enter the room.

"You have no right to be here!" Tauma sprang to his feet but was pushed back into his seat by a guard.

"No, Professor Tauma," Sana replied, walking towards the Director. "I have every right, as you well know. I will take what I have come for, which is the technology these creatures are withholding from us."

"You have gone mad," Tauma said.

Sana ignored him and surveyed the pairs at the table, the Nyrians next to their human partners, and pursed his lips.

"Captain," he said to Inessa. "Your crew will be welcome at the institute where we can work together in a more appropriate setting. We will require access to your shuttle and your ship, so that we can study and share your magnificent creations."

"We have come in peace, and you have answered with violence," Inessa said. She remained in her seat as a Nyrian approached, and watched as another collected the wrist pads on the table.

"Come now, Captain," Sana answered. "You have not acted peaceably. You have withheld and hoarded knowledge that can benefit all Nyrians. That is an aggressive act, as even Professor Tauma knows."

"As I said, you and your crew will be welcomed at the Institute. I look forward to working with you," he added. "One human is missing," he said to a guard. "Find him."

"Professor Sana," Inessa said. "Your actions could damage relations between our two peoples. I strongly suggest you rethink what you are doing."

"The damage you mention has already been done, and it is not by my hand," he replied.

Sana stepped back and clasped his hands behind his back. "Please," he said. "Finish your meal while we wait for your colleague. I am sure he will be found soon."

"I am sorry I have led you into this," Inessa said without looking up.

"We all chose to land, Captain," Gunther said.

"How are you doing, Dave?" she asked.

"I'm okay," he answered, touching his cheek.

"How long before our friend might join us?" she asked quietly.

"Three hours," Dave said. "Maybe sooner."

"I taught Hylva how to make these swirls," Gunther said. "Or she taught me how to make them with what Nyria has to offer as ingredients. I suggest we enjoy them slowly, savor them, and our time together."

"Your tablet is glowing," Ceera said.

Alan groaned, turned over and placed his pillow over his head.

"It looks very angry," she added. She nudged him with a foot when he didn't reply. "I think you should get up." She used more force when he didn't reply.

"Ow!"

"I think you should get up," Ceera said.

Alan groaned again and climbed over her naked body. His feet touched the heated floor and he slipped on some tracksuit pants. He walked to the table where his tablet glowed, glanced at the coffee, but addressed the device first. He swiped the first message, then the second, and the third, before remembering to breathe. He reviewed each of the eleven messages slowly. Most were simple, sent automatically: device deactivation, control of key systems transferred to your device, location at … Each gave coordinates of the radio transmitting station, pinpointing their location to within ten centimeters. They were all at the same place.

He swiped to the message from Inessa, and sat down as he began to read. It was terse and direct, consisting of eight words and links to programs: *Compound occupied. Crew detained. Utilize all means necessary.*

He didn't hear Ceera approach from behind and was startled when she spoke. "What does it say?" she asked.

"Nothing good," he answered, swiping to the largest message, from Dave.

We are soon to be captured by intruders. Possibly Sana, Dave wrote. *I am transferring total control of reactors on* Sunspot *and shuttle to your device. That includes self-destruct protocol, which you must use if capture is imminent. We are buying you ...* Alan searched for more text, but the message had ended.

Alan returned to Inessa's message and accessed the links she provided. Video feeds from the compound filled his screen. He flicked from camera to camera. The image of one of the small houses the Nyrians lived in, followed by another. He peered closer at the feed and saw the door to the house broken, leaning inwards. Alan continued to swipe, stopping at the camera overlooking the shuttle. A group of Nyrians clustered around the ship. He pinched and opened his fingers above the screen and the image magnified. He didn't recognize them, each dressed in black, some holding cylindrical tubes that he recognized as weapons. He pinched and opened again and watched as two tried to pry open the shuttle door.

He swiped the screen and saw the central building used for meetings and shared meals. Two armed Nyrians stood at the entrance. Alan opened the homing program activated by his captain and it pulsed from inside the building.

"What is happening?" Ceera persisted.

"The compound has been taken over," Alan said. "I've been given control of all systems. I got a message from Inessa and Dave. Then all the devices went dead."

"What does that mean?" she asked.

"I don't know," Alan admitted. "They are all in the hall. Dave thinks its Sana."

"What should we do?" she asked.

"I don't know," Alan answered.

"We should return," Ceera said, already pulling on clothes.

"Yes," he agreed.

She placed a hand on his back when he failed to get up. "Come," she said. "Let us prepare."

Ceera hurriedly put some of her clothing into a bag, saw Alan still staring mutely at his device, swiping slowly at the screen, so she filled another bag with some of his belongings. She added personal items, all the small things they brought for their stay. She put on her boots and dragged the bags out to the vehicle. She had to clamber over a drift of snow to reach it. Opening the back hatch, she checked the battery connections before dumping the bags on top of them. Moving to the driver's seat she turned the vehicle on and the engine began to quietly purr. She left the vehicle engine idling and located a snow shovel in the small garage and set to digging away at the snow drift so they could leave.

Alan swiped again, accessing the camera outside Ceera's small house. The door was ajar and the lights were on. A shadow passed a window and he made the image larger. A dark clad figure left the house, with two others close behind. He tried to follow the party but they moved out of range of the fixed lens. He swiped again, and an empty snow-covered lane filled the screen. Moving his finger across the screen another time he saw another lane, this time with the three Nyrians, walking away and again disappearing out of range of the camera.

He gave up trying to follow them and scanned the compound, one screen at a time. He returned to the shuttle. The Nyrians outside were still prying at the door. Alan accessed the shuttle through the permissions sent and images from inside the craft appeared. The door was secure, designed to withstand forces much greater than aliens with crowbars. He scrolled through shuttle systems—life support, AI, piloting, reactor. He opened reactor controls and saw that, though quiet, it was merely resting. Alan touched the screen gently and saw output increase. He touched again and brought the reading back to a state of rest.

Accessing another program, he viewed the *Sunspot*, each screen he accessed revealing another essential control of the ship. He quickly moved from station to station before stopping at the probe bay. One remained unused; a redundancy stored in case any of the three probes dedicated to scientific research malfunctioned. Alan remotely powered up the spare probe and programmed in a course. It lifted from its cradle and made its way to the airlock. Doors behind it sealed shut and those in front opened, revealing the moon below. The image was so stable that Alan didn't notice when it left the *Sunspot* and began its descent.

"The vehicle is ready," Ceera said. Alan continued to stare at his device, moving only a finger. He flinched when she touched him.

"Everything is ready," she repeated.

"Ah, good," he answered.

"We can go now," she added.

"Yes," he said. "Let's go."

19

Ceera guided the vehicle over the frozen road, her eyes focused on the small area of snow illuminated by the headlights. She rubbed her tired eyes as they approached the compound. Alan looked up from time to time, but mostly sat with his head down and his attention on his tablet. After the probe entered the atmosphere and descended to lower elevations, he initiated the dispersal sequence as the vague plan he formulated at the cabin took shape. A dozen smaller probes emerged from the belly of the larger probe and spread out around it. The viewscreen showed little in the darkness above the clouds so he worked with coordinates, guiding the little fleet to the same location they were driving to.

Snow ground beneath the tires as Ceera brought the vehicle to a stop on a small rise above the compound. Alan looked at her to signal he was ready, but his grim expression made her hesitate.

"Do not act with anger, my love," she said. "Anger will impair you."

"Oh, I'm not angry," he said, hearing it himself as he spoke.

"I will be angry for both of us," she said, carefully placing a hand on his leg. "My friends and colleagues are down there. They are my family. As are your friends and colleagues. My home is down there. And my own people are keeping them against their will. I will carry that shame, and I will carry our anger. Keep your mind clear and help those we love. Please."

She lifted her free hand to his face and stroked his cheek, lowering it when his features softened. She turned, grabbed a bag of their belongings and opened her door. He got out. They emerged into the cold, walked to the front of the vehicle and stood in the headlights, gazing down at the buildings below. Snow crunched beneath their boots as they neared the settlement, her hands curled into fists and held at her side, his holding the tablet, guiding probes to targets as they appeared. He directed the primary probe to the main hall and let it hover above the building.

He activated the audio and spoke, his voice booming over the surrounding area. "Return to your transports and leave this station now," he said. "You are in breach of the understanding reached between our people. You will release those you hold and evacuate this area immediately."

Alan held the device close to Ceera and she repeated the message in Nyrian for the benefit of any without a translator device.

"That ought to get their attention," he said.

They continued walking down the hill and the first Nyrians appeared. They stood to the left of the main hall, raised their weapons and Ceera and Alan stopped. Alan touched an icon on the tablet and a small drone descended, buzzing the Nyrians as it flew past and exploded with a blinding flash a short distance away. He touched the screen again and another drone swooped to the right and over the heads of Nyrian guards there. Another flash of light lit the scene as it exploded behind them.

"Lower your weapons, and depart this area," he said, his voice once again amplified.

The Nyrians backed away slowly. Alan examined the image of the shuttle through a small drone hovering above. A small party of Nyrians stood near, their efforts to enter the shuttle blunted. Alan accessed the reactor and increased power. Utilizing the pilot controls, he activated propulsion. Snow rapidly melted around the rear of the craft as propellant began to escape. He increased power from two percent to three, the glow from the stern lighting the scene an eerie yellow. He stopped after the Nyrian party ran away from the ship.

Returning his attention to the main hall, he spoke again. "Sana," he said. "Order your men to stand down. Release my crew and the Nyrians with them. Return to your vehicles and leave this station."

Alan and Ceera reached level ground in front of the main entrance, the compacted snow crunching underfoot. Alan sensed movement in the shadows beside them and saw three Nyrians moving close. He touched the screen and a small drone swooped down. It hovered above them as Alan directed it in a slow circle an arm's length above their head. They glanced nervously up and Alan guided the probe twenty meters away before making it self-destruct in a blinding explosion. The Nyrians threw themselves in the ground, covering their heads. As silence descended once again, they rose sheepishly, still holding their weapons, but the dangerous end pointing at the snow near their feet.

Alan and Ceera turned their attention to movement at the entrance of the main hall. Sana stepped out of the door, flanked by two armed guards. He took several steps away from the door and stopped.

"You cannot stop us, Atmospheric Scientist Alan Reading," he said. "You will hand over control of your technology for our study, and you will accompany me and your colleagues to the Institute where the real collaboration between our species will commence."

"Who does this son of a bitch think he is?" Alan said to Ceera.

"Let me carry our anger, my love, "she said. "Get our family out of there."

Alan took a deep breath and exhaled slowly. "I repeat," Alan said through speakers on the large probe hidden in the dark above. "Return to your transports and leave this station now. You are in breach of the understanding between our people. Release those you hold and evacuate this area immediately."

Sana motioned the guards. As they stepped forward, Alan guided the larger probe lower until it hovered directly above Sana. Holding the tablet above his head, Alan walked towards the Nyrians.

"Above us is the mother probe," he said without amplification. "Each of the smaller probes is equipped with enough explosives to destroy itself if anybody tries to tamper with it. This is done so technology does not fall into uninvited hands. The probe above is also equipped with explosives. Lots of explosives. It is programmed to self-destruct. If it were to explode right now, it would level this entire area. This building. Those guards. You. Me."

"Nonsense!" Sana said.

"I can't let you have any technology. The shuttle is also programmed to self-destruct. We're lucky your men didn't get in."

"You would not kill yourself and your crew," Sana said.

"If you don't leave, I don't have a choice," Alan replied.

"Take him," Sana ordered the guards. They glanced at the probe hovering above their heads, and then at their superior.

"Do you know what I am holding?" Alan asked. "It's the dead man's switch. If my hand comes away from this tablet, the probe above you will self-destruct."

He motioned to Ceera who spoke to the guards. Any guard without a device now understood what they were standing under. They glanced at Sana and made no attempt to subdue Alan.

"You don't want me to let go of this device," Alan said, waiting for Ceera to repeat before continuing. "The shuttle will also self-destruct. That explosion will reduce the entire station to rubble."

"You bluff," Sana said.

"Unfortunately, that's not true," Alan said. He looked at Ceera and smiled softly before returning to meet Sana's eyes. "I wish there was another way. But there isn't. Please leave with your men. I don't want to die as much as you."

"You lie," Sana said, hands on hips, but his face gave him away.

"Very well," Alan replied. He walked closer to the front door, ignoring Sana and his men. "Captain," he called, "You can come out now. The shuttle is prepped for departure."

"You are going nowhere!" Sana shouted.

He flinched as Alan brought the tablet closer and touched it with his right hand. Alan made a small circular motion and the distant shuttle's engine began to growl. The guards next to Sana stepped farther away. Sana stepped forward and Alan touched the screen again, causing a small probe to explode to the left. Sana stood still and let Inessa, Trauma and the others exited the building. Inessa nodded to Alan as she continued to stride in the direction of the shuttle. Alan programmed two small probes to follow the party, encouraging any reluctant Nyrian guards to move away from the entourage.

Ceera placed a hand on Alan's shoulder. He held the tablet towards the Nyrians, and when he was certain his unspoken message was received, he and Ceera followed the others to the shuttle. Without turning around, he could hear Sana and the guards following a short distance behind. Alan made a small drone hover behind him, circling and swooping in the darkness. The larger probe followed above at their walking pace, its propellers quietly slicing the air.

At the shuttle, several of Sana's guards stood at a safe distance. They made no effort to stop the party. Alan accessed the shuttle program and opened the door that the Nyrians had tried to pry open. It smoothly shifted to the side and the ramp descended. Maria entered first, making her way directly to the pilot's seat. Nola entered with her and stood awkwardly in the passenger cabin. Inessa helped her to sit in a chair, adjusting the safety straps and buckling her in before sitting Tauma in her own seat. The other humans copied their captain and guided their Nyrian partner to a chair. Alan retracted the ramp behind him and Ceera and closed the door, sealing them in. He looked around the crowded shuttle. All the seats were occupied and the human crew stood and stared at him.

"Alright, Alan," Maria called back. "I'd like my ship back, if you don't mind."

Alan pursed his lips as he tried to make sense of what she said, breathed out and shook his head. He still had complete and sole access to all programs. He swiped the screen of his tablet and returned the piloting controls to Maria.

"All yours," he called forward.

"Alan," Dave said. "If you wouldn't mind."

"And I can take the probes now," Gunther said. "You've done well for an atmospheric specialist, but time to let the professionals work."

"He has done very well," Inessa added. "Thank you, Alan. And thank you Ceera. But it is time we go. Ensure you are secure. I have a feeling this take off will be bumpy."

Crew wedged themselves in front and beside the seats as the ship began vibrating. Alan finished returning system controls to their rightful owners, stowed the bag Ceera carried, put his tablet in a pocket and sat at the rear of the cabin. He wrapped his arms around Ceera as she sat between his legs.

"Hold on to my arms," he told her. "And brace your legs against the back of that seat. Everything is going to be alright."

The shuttle tilted upwards as Maria fired the bow thrusters. Ceera slid back into Alan, and he felt the cold steel of the bulkhead behind him push into his back as the ship left the surface. Ceera's head pressed against his chest and he tried to bend and kiss it, instead satisfying himself with burying his nose in her hair and taking in her aroma. All sound was cancelled with the vibration and thrust of the shuttle as it rose from the surface. Alan breathed out as the shuttle leveled off and flew above the clouds.

Snippets of conversation drifted in.

"You can destroy it all?" Alan heard Tauma ask. "It is true the probe is a bomb?"

"Yes," Gunther answered. "Not a bomb, just a precaution—"

"You can destroy it all?" Tauma asked again.

"Yes," Gunther replied.

"Then do it," Tauma said. "Wipe it away. Do not let him have it."

"The explosion will kill any in the vicinity," Gunther said.

"Then they die," Tauma said.

"Do you really want that?" Inessa asked. "You are not a murderer."

"He has taken everything from me," Tauma said. "He deserves what he gets."

"You are not a killer," Inessa said. Alan had never heard his captain plead before. But there was more in her voice that was new to him. She was seeing the character of the man she loved being tested, and she was scared of the outcome. He could feel her relief at his response.

"Then what can you do?" he asked.

"I can delay the explosion," Gunther said. "Give them time to leave."

"Time? He doesn't deserve time."

"I am thinking about his men," Gunther answered. "They are only following orders."

"Of course," Tauma said.

"Captain?" Gunther asked.

"A warning," Inessa said. "Just enough time to escape the blast, if they start running now. Then detonate."

The probe hovered above the large radio telescope that transmitted the Nyrian message across space. Gunther programmed the probe to emit a warning giving those in the vicinity two minutes to escape the imminent blast, followed by a very loud countdown. Silence filled the shuttle as seconds ticked away, until a glow from the explosion illuminated the clouds below. The radio disc, and the small settlement, were consumed in flames when the probe self-destructed. Alan pressed his face against Ceera's and it was wetted by her tears. He held her tighter.

"Sana will never let me be free," Tauma said to Inessa.

"Even after you let him live?" Inessa asked.

"Especially because I let him live," Tauma said. "He will search for us, thinking we have the secrets he covets." *And he will find us*, Tauma admitted, but only to himself.

"I want to take you home," Inessa said.

"But you cannot," Tauma answered. "There is no space on your ship, you have told me there are only twelve chairs, and no others can travel," Tauma said. "You will return to your home, and we will stay in ours."

Alan wanted to plug his ears, to not overhear his captain and her lover's conversation, to not be a part of the truth they were having to face, that he had to face. He waited for an objection from his captain, a rebuttal, a solution. But none came.

"You must set us down near a city, I will tell you which one," Tauma continued. "We will fade into the collective, make new identities, play new roles. We will survive and live out our lives. And you will return to your home safely. That is what matters most to me. That you will be okay."

"I will not be okay," Inessa said. "I will be dead inside."

"You will be alive," Tauma said. "And you will know that I love you, even if I am far away. Please, you must live for us."

Ceera's body shuddered against Alan's as she sobbed quietly. He tightened his arms around her, not knowing of anything else to do, and cried quietly with her.

20

Maria set the shuttle down outside of a medium-sized city, darkness and cloud masking their arrival. The door opened and ramp descended, and the passengers slowly disembarked, leaving the ship in pairs, walking slowly, as if injured or disorientated. Which they were, in their separate ways. Alan helped Ceera to her feet, and walked down the ramp with his arm around her. She clutched the satchel she brought from the hut, nestled in the mountains so far away. Hours had passed since they left, but it felt like days.

Snow fell gently, quiet surrounding them. Ceera reached into the bag and withdrew a book wrapped in cloth. She handed it to Alan.

"No," he said.

"You must take it," she said. "It is too precious to leave."

"You are too precious to leave," he choked.

"Please, Alan," she pleaded. "To remember us."

He pushed the book back towards her. "I gave it to you. Keep it. Let it be a memory you keep for both of us."

She gave in and clutched the small bundle to her breast before kneeling and putting it back into the satchel. She felt around in the bag and stood, offering her closed hand to Alan. Opening it, she revealed a small, smooth stone. He knew it immediately. It was egg shaped and polished by many hours of handling, carried in her own hand as she travelled, a small and secret companion in her isolation, a small act of rebellion against the collective, an intimate private and personal possession in a world where everything was shared. Alan took it and wrapped his fingers around it.

"Thank you," he said.

He held it as the snow continued to fall. They gazed at each other, in a place beyond words, unable to speak and not really wanting to. Alan stepped closer and Ceera fell into his arms, and they stayed that way, motionless and speechless. Around them similar scenes played out. Some cried, some struggled, but not for long. They all realized their time was short, and used what was left with words or actions that were more important.

"I was whole," Ceera said into Alan's shoulder. "I am whole, because of you. I never dreamed that I would ever feel complete. But you complete me."

"I want to stay," Alan said. "We can live at the cabin—"

"No, we cannot. Nowhere will be safe. And you know that," Ceera said.

"I—"

"No, Alan," Ceera said, pulling away and meeting his eyes. "You will go, and you will live. And you will take me with you, here." She placed her hand on his heart. He put his hand over hers.

"That is where we will always be together," she said.

They stood that way, hands on each other's heart, drowning in each other's eyes, and oblivious to the sound of feet approaching.

"Come, we must go. The longer we stay, the more danger we place them in," Inessa said behind them. Then she moved on to other couples and repeated the message.

Ceera moved back from Alan, took his hand and guided him to the waiting shuttle. She stopped when they reached the ramp and let go. He stood mutely looking at the ramp until Ceera gently pushed him forward. He took a numbed step, and then another. He turned to see her, her mouth quivering.

"Please," said. "Go my love, my heart."

"I have no life without you," Alan said.

"Please, my love. Live for us."

Alan stood on the ramp, staring, unmoving.

"Please," her words urged him. "I live with you. In you. Go for us both."

Alan turned and walked up the remainder of the ramp. He entered the shuttle, somehow found his seat and strapped in as his crewmates did likewise. He watched Maria walk to the pilot's chair and the controls. The craft vibrated and tilted as its bow rose in preparation for lift off. The hum of the reactor filled Alan's ears and his body shook with its power as the ship rose from the surface and gained altitude. Alan closed his eyes and cried, uselessly protesting, trying to stop the momentum carrying them upward with the power of his pain. But it wasn't enough. The shuttle rose through snow and cloud, until the naked night sky revealed a galaxy of stars, until even the thin air of the upper atmosphere gave way to the vacuum and black of space. Maria programmed a course to the *Sunspot*, put her face and her hands, and wept as the computer guided the shuttle back to its home.

The crew disembarked and prepared for acceleration in their own numb silence. Alan watched Inessa's mouth move, issuing unnecessary orders or words of encouragement. Prepare stations, check systems, assist ... He ran through safety checks on the reactor under Dave's supervision, consisting primarily of points and nods of the head. Alan felt a prick on his arm and noticed he was in the sickbay being examined by Shu Len. Her eyes were unusual in that they were alert, seeming to take in the entire crew, rather than the task at hand or the system they were responsible for. The entire crew was her area of responsibility, the collective organism her system to check. Alan watched her mouth move and heard her words through a haze of grief.

"I am going to need you. Stay with me."

He smiled weakly and nodded, not fully comprehending what she said. Hours passed, which may have been minutes. Or minutes in hours. He secured his quarters and dressed in the paper gown and diaper for acceleration. Opening his palm, he studied the smooth stone, a memory from a distant place and moment. He wiped tears with his free hand, looked around the small room for a secure place, and finally settled on the sheepskin slippers nestled below his bunk. Reaching into one, he placed the stone inside. He headed to his acceleration couch, climbed onto it and placed his arms on the cushioned rests. He stared at a small space on the bulkhead, oblivious to those around him, the jab from the needle as the final acceleration drugs were administered, or the weight increasing as the *Sunspot* fled from Nyria, towards its sun, and earth.

After first acceleration, Alan rose, walked to the waste chut and deposited his soiled garments. He stood in line behind Maria, awaited his turn in the shower, and washed. It was habit that guided him, muscle memory, or a small part of his mind that still felt there was a reason to carry on. In the messroom Shu Len moved about the crew, checking blood pressure or pupil response, encouraging fluid and food intake, administering drugs as she deemed necessary, primarily anti-depressants both chemical and cannabinoid. Alan felt a prick in his arm and Shu Len's breath on his face as she knelt close and spoke into his ear.

"You are doing well," she said. "We will make it home and carry them with us, here." She put her hand over his heart and pressed gently.

And then he was sitting in his acceleration couch again, weight crushing his chest, the small spot on the bulkhead filled with Ceera's face, the sadness and loss in her eyes. He stared into them as they moved across the ceiling, wanting to let the darkness lurking in the periphery consume him, take him, yet keeping that escape at bay, choosing instead the continued torment and torture he felt he deserved.

Suddenly the world lightened and he floated against the restraining straps. A needle pierced his arm and he gulped in air, his eyes widening. Pain raced across his face as Shu Len slapped him.

"I said, assistance required! Now move yourself," she growled.

Alan fumbled at his straps and propelled himself from his chair, crashing into the couch next to his before steadying himself. His eyes darted around the room, searching for Shu Len. She bent over Abede and he joined her.

"CPR. Start now," she ordered.

Alan began rhythmically pushing on the center of Abede's chest. Shu Len pushed him away a moment later and stabbed Abede's chest with an injector, watched for a moment, and barked again.

"Continue!"

Alan kept pushing, losing count and sensation in his arms. Finally, Shu Len pushed him aside, ripped away Abede's acceleration gown and placed a defibrillator on his chest. Small droplets of blood emerged as its claws dug into the man's skin.

"Step away," Shu Len said as she activated the box. Abede convulsed, his back arching. His eyes opened and he gulped air, his desperate breathing turning into sobs when he realized he was back on the ship.

"Keep him with us," Shu Len told Alan. "I will assess the others," she added, moving away from the pair.

"Why?" Abede asked once they were alone.

"Orders, man," Alan said, placing a palm against the other man's face. "You have to stay with us. We're all going home. We owe them that much."

"Ranna," Abede whispered. But Alan couldn't hear what he said. He just let his crewmate cry as the monitor attached to his chest beeped.

Alan had a dim memory of all the crew sitting around the long table in the messroom, drinks growing cold in front of them. No words were spoken, at least none that he remembered. Gunther sat next to Inessa, staring at his hands. The middle of the table was empty—no German pastries, no speeches. Even Jardin sat silently. Nobody wanted to hear his preemptory apology, and many didn't mind if he failed. They drifted away from the table, to their stations for final preparations to fold time and space and return to their own time and place.

He felt a prick as the medic injected a pre-acceleration concoction, and his vision narrowed as consciousness was funneled to a fine point filled with a reminder of what was left behind. Ceera's face again moved across the ceiling as the hours passed, and the *Sunspot* passed through the Nyrian star, emerging in Earth's solar system. Alan felt the moment, lifting as the gravity of acceleration left him as the reactor ceased its incessant push and the ship rotated, a brief moment filled with panic and confusion, before the weight of deceleration crashed on him, reminding his bruised mind where he was. His view narrowed again, and he stared into the memory of Ceera's eyes.

"Assistance required!" Shu Len shouted.

The sound of the medic's voice bounced off the walls and bulkheads. Alan struggled with his straps, with freeing himself and forcing his numbed legs to carry him to where she stood. He looked down at his captain. Her eyes were closed and her mouth rested in a faint smile. He had never seen such serene beauty on a face and stood hypnotized by it.

"Do your job!" Shu Len barked, before searching her supplies for an injector.

Alan reached down and tore away Inessa's paper gown, revealing her breasts. He punched her in the chest. Her body shook, but her face remained calm. He hit her again, and when her heart refused to respond, he pressed repeatedly until Shu Len shoved him aside and attached the defibrillator. Its feet dug into her skin and she grimaced as the device sent a jolt of electricity into her heart. Shu Len stepped closer and examined the readings on the machine, satisfied at the consistency of the rhythm. Alan looked down at Inessa, her face now a mask of pain. She opened her eyes and met his, her vision blurred by the tears already forming.

"Come," Shu Len ordered. "She isn't the only one."

She grabbed Alan by the arm and pulled him to another couch where Gunther lay. Alan tore his gown and punched the probe controller's chest, and pressed repeatedly when there was no response.

"After two minutes, attach and activate defibrillator," Shu Len said. "I will see to Maria."

Alan counted with each press before losing place, and when his arms burned from the effort he stopped and located the device. Placing it on Jardin's chest, he stepped back as it dug into the man and delivered its charge. Gunther gasped and gulped in air.

"Nein nein nein," he groaned.

Alan put his hand on Gunther's head and stroked his greasy hair. "We're all going home," Alan apologized. "All of us."

At the sound of her voice, Alan turned and started moving towards Shu Len.

"Assistance required!" she shouted.

21

Captain Todd Nichols thanked his medical officer and made his way to the wash station. He dropped his gown and sanitary pad in the disposal chute and entered the shower. He felt life flow back into arms and legs as the warm water coursed down his body. Stepping out, he toweled off, put on his flight suit and joined his communications specialist on the bridge. She always reached her post before any crew, including her captain, listening intently to any transmissions in the new solar system.

"What are the locals saying?" he asked as he entered.

"News and gossip, from what I gather," Dana answered. "The computer is still processing changes in the linguistic structure."

"Okay," Nichols replied, waiting for her to answer his unasked question.

"No mention of us," she said, satisfying his query. "I think there is a disturbance in an urban center, and a strong response by the local authorities, but until I can translate fully, it's just conjecture. Most of what I am hearing is ... well, the language I am hearing is definitely different from the original transmission, but not unrecognizable. Give me a couple days and I'll crack it."

"I can do that," Nichols said, sitting down in the captain's chair. "We have sixty hours until next decel." He gazed at the ringed gas giant in the viewscreen, and the smaller planet orbiting it, seen as a bright light from the distance of the *Solar Flare*.

"It's very beautiful," he said.

"Very," Dana agreed, taking off her earphones. She leaned back in her chair and gazed at the screen with her captain until they were interrupted.

"That's a mighty fine picture," Lawson said as he entered the bridge.

"It is indeed," Nichols answered without turning away from the screen. "And that was some mighty fine astrogating, Lieutenant Commander."

"Just doing my job, Captain," Lawson replied.

"Take the complement, Dennis," Nichols said. "Are the crew assembled?"

"That is what I came to report," Lawson answered. "McAlister had a blood vessel burst in his calf, but Berger patched him up. She said he'll be fine for the next decel with extra compression bandages. But everyone's assembled and waiting."

Nichols acknowledged with a nod before moving carefully in the micro-gravity, past the astrogator and first mate and down the hall to the messroom. Lawson and Dana followed him into the common-room and took their assigned seats.

"We have entered the Nyrian solar system," Nichols began addressing his crew. "I congratulate your professionalism and competence in taking us this far. We have evidence that Nyria is an advanced civilization, and I look forward to what our science team will learn about this planet. Communication Specialist Rice is analyzing the current Nyrian language structure and we will soon be able to decipher all of the communications emanating from the planet."

Nichols smiled at his crew before motioning to atmospheric specialist, Greg Owen, in the galley. Owen made his way forward, holding a box in front of him. The captain stopped him, took the box and placed it on the table. He lifted a bottle out and showed it to his crew so they could see the familiar red and white label and read the name they all recognized.

"Tabitha will say you should only drink water, and you will hydrate as the doctor orders," the captain said with a wink towards his medical officer. "But first enjoy a cold beer. You have crossed space. You are in a new solar system, with a new world before us. We have a job to complete, and I'm confident you'll perform your duties with the utmost professionalism. But first, you deserve a bottle, and here it is."

Owen passed the beer around the table, each received gratefully. Caps were twisted off and bottles raised to their captain before they drank.

"To you," Nichols said. "Who have sailed to a new world."

He paused and looked thoughtfully at the ceiling, as if peering through the bulkhead and into space. "And to Nyria," he added, "whoever you might be."

Nichols opened his eyes as the stimulants revived him. He felt the oppressive weight of deceleration lift but there was no relief. His ears were assaulted with a sound that acted like a spike being driven into his brain, hammering away, followed by a screeching wail, and then the spike again. He swung his feet to deck and forced himself to stand. He lurched forward and fell on top of the chair of his first mate. Lawson was the astrogator, but he was also head of security. For some reason this was important. Nichols' ears became numbed by the sound attacking them, but his mind was becoming clearer. His hands found the medical controls they sought and he administered a shot of stimulants into Lawson's tired body. The astrogator's eyes shot open and the face of his captain filled his entire view.

Nichols shouted at the man below him as the hammering and screeching suddenly made sense and his mind caught up with trained actions. "Proximity alert! The ship is being boarded."

Nichols pushed away from the chair and crashed into the next as Lawson left his and rushed to his team, injecting emergency stimulant into the first and moving to the next. The medic, Tabitha Berger, monitored crew by sight as they rose from their chairs and made their way to their emergency stations. She watched Lawson drag the drone controller, Sam McAlister, and the xeno-biologist, Ancia Prock, to the armory. Prock looked confused and pale, no doubt dehydrated, disorientated and in shock, but mobile, which was all that was required in what might be a combat situation.

The medic turned her attention to the co-pilot, Andrea Turner, who remained in her chair. Without checking vitals, she brought a fist down on her chest. Berger could feel the tendons ripping as sternum tried to tear away from rib, but she stuck again. She put her ear next to Turner's mouth and nose, trying to feel breath, but none came.

"Assistance required!" the medic shouted as she commenced chest compressions, doing for the heart what it should have been doing for itself.

When nobody shouldered her aside to take her place and allow her to do her job, she looked around to see an empty room. She left her patient and retrieved the defibrillator, ripped away Turner's paper gown and placed the device on her bare breast. Claws dug into her flesh and the medic stepped back as a jolt of electricity was administered. She waited for a pulse to register but none did. Another jolt caused

Turner to involuntarily arch before she fell back into her chair and began gasping for breath.

Berger watched for a moment, wanting to reassure or comfort, but instead turned away, grabbed her bag, and left the room by pushing off of Turner's chair. She headed towards noise coming from the direction of the reactor room, immediately adapting to the total absence of gravity. The ship had stopped spinning, and even the microgravity that rotation produced was gone. Berger had never experienced cessation of rotation on a mission, but she knew it could not mean anything good. She propelled herself down the passageway, keeping her body as close to the floor as possible. Her actions were instinctual, from countless hours of training. At the corner of the passageway leading to the reactor she tapped the deck, rose slightly and grabbed a handhold, stopping her momentum with a painful crash into the wall. Her eyes captured the scene in the brief moment before she pushed lightly off the handhold and drifted back the way she came. She analyzed what she saw.

In combat triage, Lawson was code black. The gaping wound in his chest, the cloud of blood surrounding his body, the listlessness of limbs meant that he was dead. Berger cursed her training and its indications and lists. In the fraction of a moment that she lingered in the corridor, she peered into Lawson's lifeless eyes and knew everything. There were no lists to describe the condition of Prock. The xeno-botanist's headless body floated against the ceiling. McAlister was still breathing, but he was missing a leg and his face betrayed hypovolemic shock. He was losing too much blood. She brought up the image of his face, the glaze in his pleading eyes, and made a battlefield decision.

She abandoned the crew where they were, pushed against the wall, and made her way to the redoubt position. The bridge held control for all systems, from reactor to life support. Berger moved closer to the deck as she floated forward. She turned sideways so she could see as she passed the messroom. Through several pairs legs and booted feet, she caught a glimpse of the face of the atmospheric specialist. Owen stared at something or someone near him, a figure obscured by table and chair. The medic analyzed Owen's face before concentrating on the immediate. More words in a list: fear, surprise, anger, pain. She wondered briefly who else might be in the room with him. The mess was muster station for the science team, Tony Glen, the xeno-geologist and Cynthia Long, the xeno-linguist. All except for Prock, who came from special forces before specializing in botany.

Berger rose from the floor as she approached the bridge. She reached out for a handhold to steady herself, to allow a recon, to allow for quick retreat. She grabbed the hold, and took in the corridor. The bridge door was open. A figure stood in its entrance, looking right at her. He held a cylindrical device she knew was a weapon. She felt the bulkhead slam into her back, and red fluid floated in the air in front of her. She felt nothing, but knew everything. She touched her chest and looked at her hands, covered in her own blood. She moved her head down to see the wound, but her vision darkened and she was consumed by a blackness darker than space. Before she was lost in complete emptiness she saw the face of her killer, and her last thought was of the color of an ice cream she ate as a child, and the taste of cold raspberry. Then her hand released its grip and her body drifted in the corridor.

Nichols surveyed the bridge and knew his ship was lost. Skip Turietta floated near his station. Nichols didn't know if the pilot was still alive. The shot outside the entrance told him there was no escape. He saw the fear in the communication specialist's eyes standing next to him, but her face was an iron mask of indignation and resistance. He admired her strength, and he mirrored it, leading by example.

Staring at the alien in front of him he added words to his look. "You have no right attacking my ship and crew!" Nichols growled.

The alien responded by emitting a menacing screech that sounded like a bird of prey on the attack. Dana and Nichols caught each other's eye before they were both grabbed roughly, their heads bent to the side, and a small translator device shoved down their ear canals. The screeching stopped.

" ... access to your reactor, now!" the alien said.

"I am Captain Todd Nichols of the interstellar exploratory ship, *Solar Flare*. We are on a peaceful mission to respond—"

Nichols' face exploded in pain. His body hit the bulkhead behind him before a hand caught his wrist and jerked him back to an upright position in front of what he could only assume was a Nyrian. He looked at his own body, naked except for where remnants of his paper gown still clung, and sanitary briefs saturated with urine. It didn't cut a very intimidating picture. He took hold of the console beside him before pulling his hand out of the grip of the Nyrian near him.

"I am Captain Todd Nichols of the—" was all he managed to get out before being struck again. He maintained his hold on the console so did not drift from his position.

"You will give me access to your reactors immediately," the Nyrian standing before him demanded.

"I can't do that!" Nichols responded, and braced himself for the strike that followed. He spat out blood which drifted away from his face.

"He can't transfer control!" Dana shouted.

The Nyrian turned towards her and raised his hand as if to strike. "We don't have the ability to transfer control!" she added.

The pleading tone of her voice gave the Nyrian pause. He looked at the species from across the galaxy, beings he thought were mere myth.

Yet he, and others in the military collective, had been waiting all the same for their prophesized return, and their storied power over time and space. It was an old story, of a failed invasion of powerful aliens, naively invited by outcast Nyrians, and finally chased from the planet, disappearing into the dark from whence they came.

The frail beings in front of him did not seem to convey the existential threat that he was raised to believe. He was taught to fear the beings from afar, but he was not afraid. Despite her postering, the female let her fear show in her eyes. She might be malleable. The male not only hid his fear, it was practically absent. Unlike the female, he already knew he was dead. The Nyrian struck him with a closed fist to wipe the defiant look from his face. The human calling himself Captain Todd Nichols fell back, regained his position, spat more blood and glared at the Nyrian. It didn't matter. He was useless now.

"Who controls the reactor?" the Nyrian directed his question at Rice.

"She does not—"

Nichols didn't see the strike coming and was not prepared. The force propelled him against the bulkhead where his head hit with a dull clunk, and he floated across the bridge, unconscious.

"My name is Dana Rice, communication specialist of the interstellar ship, *Solar Flare*. We are on a—"

"Delay will only prolong your pain, Communication Specialist Dana Rice," the Nyrian interrupted. He withdrew a black oblong shape from a pocket, squeezed it in his fist, and a barbed blade clicked out of it.

"Who controls the reactor?" the Nyrian asked.

"My name is Dana Rice—"

She screamed as the blade tore through the flesh of her hip, ripping pieces off as it was withdrawn. She instinctively reached for her wound, but her hands were held by guards.

"Who controls the reactor?" he asked again.

Dana began to cry. He knew he was close, that her façade was nearing collapse.

"My name is—"

The Nyrian stabbed again, ripping away flesh from the other hip. The human female screamed in pain, and began to cry. He stabbed again without bothering to question, a sharp thrust to her thigh. She screamed again, and he let her sob for a moment before continuing his interrogation.

"Who controls the reactor?" he asked, almost gently.

"Ron O'Brien is the reactor technician," she replied. "But he—"

The Nyrian didn't let her finish. His hand shot out and the blade pierced Rice's heart. He turned, not bothering to look into the human's shocked eyes as she realized she was dead, and he issued an order.

"Bring the human called Ron O'Brien," he said. "Dispose of the rest."

O'Brien appeared on the bridge, a Nyrian gripping each of his arms. His paper gown was soaked with blood, none of it his. He saw his captain floating unconscious, the pilot and communication specialist clearly dead. His captors stopped their momentum in front of a Nyrian he could only assume was their commander. O'Brien's head was jerked to the side and a translator bud shoved into his ear.

"You are the reactor technician?" the Nyrian asked.

"I am Reactor Technician Ron O'Brien of the—"

"Stop with that nonsense!" the Nyrian barked. "Give me control of the reactors."

"Not possible," O'Brien answered.

The Nyrian could see this human also knew he would not live long. He had already given up any hope of escape. In battle, that made for a fierce opponent. In interrogation, it was simply irritating.

"Control of your reactors," the Nyrian repeated. His voice was calm and dispassionate.

"Not possible," O'Brien repeated.

The Nyrian listened and watched. The human was not afraid, because he realized his imminent death and accepted it. But there was more. His response was a show of defiance, but also truth.

"Explain," the Nyrian invited.

"The reactors are biologically locked," O'Brien answered with a faint smile. "It's called a failsafe, so motherfuckers like you can't take it. Go ahead and try, and see what happens. Please. I really want you to."

The Nyrian resisted the urge to strike, and instead simply repeated, "Explain."

"Fuck you," O'Brien said.

"I access the reactor, and the reactor will be destroyed?" The Nyrian looked to another working at the astrogator's station, read the answer to his unspoken question and returned his gaze to the human.

"Oh, yeah," O'Brien answered. "And maybe half your planet. Now why don't you fuck off this ship and let us go home."

They were O'Brien's last words. The blade flashed across the short space separating them and entered his heart. The Nyrian left it protruding from his chest and turned to the Nyrian at astrogation.

"We have access to navigation," he reported. "The course back to their planet is pre-programmed."

"Will the reactor respond?"

"It appears that it will take the craft back to its origin. We can alter the program to maintain acceleration to that place," he reported. "But as the human said, any attempt to access reactor technology will result in self-destruction."

"You said, 'it appears'," the Nyrian commander replied. "Will it, or won't it?"

"My apologies, commander. The reactor will return the craft."

"Then proceed with the plan," the Nyrian ordered. "Have the device sent and deployed on board. Then send this ship back from where it came, and erase any future threat these creatures may pose to the collective."

22

Eva scanned all frequencies and got the same results. She resent the message she transmitted before final deceleration: *Sunspot approaching, arriving sector Twenty-Two-B, that is sector Twoer Twoer Bravo. Please acknowledge*. The sensors of the International Space Agency and the Interstellar Response Team should have detected the ship at first deceleration. But instead of the usual greetings and congratulations, all Eva found was silence. She resent the message: *Sunspot approaching, arriving sector Twenty-Two-B, that is, sector Twoer Twoer Bravo. Please acknowledge*.

"What is the response?" Inessa asked.

"Nothing," Eva answered.

"What else do you hear?" her captain asked.

"Nothing," Eva answered.

"That's not possible," Eva said. "What are you hearing?"

"Nothing!" Eva said, trying to restrain the annoyance she felt. It was the twentieth time her captain had asked the question. Inessa heard it, and dismissed it.

"Keep trying," she said.

"Chen, what's wrong with this picture?" she asked her astrogator across the bridge. "Where are we?"

"Just where we should be, ma'am," he answered as formally as he could manage. "We are in Sol system, exactly where we should be, fifty thousand klicks from Luna station."

"Then what's is going on? Why is there no reply?" Inessa demanded, annoyance escaping in her tone. She let it. "Damn it, where are visuals? Where are my eyes?"

"All visuals are down, Captain," Chen replied. Inessa noticed the formality from him as well. She knew the ship's scanners were down, that all they showed was static caused by an unknown radioactive source. Something was frying all external sensors. She was blind and deaf, and did not know what her ship had flown into. Snapping at her crew did not improve that situation.

"Thank you, Astrogator Chen," she said. She tried to keep her tone level to mask a growing fear. "Keep trying."

"Maria, we'll have a look the old-fashioned way," Inessa said to the pilot.

"You mean with our eyes?"

"Prep the shuttle," Inessa said. "And have Jardin and Alan there. Chen, you have the bridge. Contact me as soon as you detect anything. Or hear anything, Eva."

"Yes, ma'am," they both replied.

"And stop that," Inessa said before leaving the bridge. "I'm sorry for being such a bitch. I'm scared and freaked out, just like you. I love you. Now let's figure out what is going on."

"Yes, ma'am," they both replied again, but it meant something totally different this time.

The shuttle emerged into darkness. Maria rotated the craft and Luna lay before them. The Sea of Showers lay directly in front. Maria fired stern thrusters and the shuttle accelerated. She maneuvered and the grey surface shifted until the bright outline of Copernicus Crater spread before them. Maria magnified the image and located Luna Base. She increased magnification.

"Why is it dark?" Jardin asked from behind her.

Maria ignored him. "Luna Base, this *Sunspot* shuttle, coming in for landing. Quarantine protocol required," Maria radioed. "I repeat, quarantine protocol required. Please acknowledge. Over."

They waited in silence for a response, but none came. The shape of the base lay before them, the complex sprawling across the crater silent. The typically busy space port appeared empty.

"*Sunspot*, shuttle preparing for descent to Luna Base. Can you hail then at all? Over."

"Eva, Maria here. Pick up and respond. Over." Maria added after several seconds ticked by.

"Eva—" She left relay open and turned to Inessa. "There's nothing on any frequency," she told the captain. "Comms are fried all over out here."

"Which is what we knew on the ship," Inessa answered. "Thanks for trying," she added.

"Why is it dark?" Jardin asked again. "The station. It is dark."

Maria continued to ignore him, reacting as the helm told her to rotate the shuttle and begin deceleration for descent. She fired rotational thrusters and the moon slipped from view as the shuttle turned, pointing its stern towards Luna Base and its bow towards earth. Only after initiated landing procedures and programming the necessary reactor thrust to bring them safely to the surface did she look up and out of the front viewscreen. A whimper escaped her lips.

"*Madre de Dios*," Jardin said from behind her.

Earth filled the viewscreen, but not the earth they left. The planet tilted sharply on its axis, as if threatening to topple over. The magnificent blue of its vast oceans was gone, replaced by brown and black. The grand oasis in the lifeless expanse, home to billions, was broken. A large piece was missing, as if bitten off by some unimaginable beast. Fragments of the crust spread slowly from the gaping wound, chunks the size of continents being pulled from the planet's grasp, drifting out of its orbit. The crew in the shuttle gazed upon a shattered and lifeless world.

"*Gospodi*!" Inessa said.

They sat mute in the flight chairs, eyes glued to the scene above them. The shuttle landed, and the landing pad descended into the underground hangar. The horrific picture slowly disappeared when the shuttle sank and the ceiling closed above them. Each remained seated, staring into the darkness around them as the landing bay re-pressurized.

Inessa unstrapped and made her way to the shuttle door, she opened it and walked down the ramp. The others followed. No one spoke as they crossed the hangar, their way forward illuminated by the beams of their flashlights. Alan shone his beam around the hangar. Hair on the back of neck. When he passed through Luna Base on his way to the *Sunspot* at the beginning of the mission, the hangar was a hive of activity, with crews departing for vessels docked outside, goods being loaded and unloaded or shuttles preparing to rejoin waiting star ships orbiting the moon. Now it resembled a tomb.

He left the shadowy silence and followed Inessa through a hatchway and down a corridor. The scene was the same as the hangar. Their handheld lights provided the only illumination, the beams bouncing off the walls as they walked forward. Inessa checked her memory of the base by consulting a map mounted on the wall. A small red dot indicated where they were. She traced a route with her finger that led to a command center, then turned away and walked down the empty corridor.

They turned a corner and saw the first body. Alan held his light as Inessa knelt and examined the woman. There was no blood, no evidence of trauma. She looked as if she lay down in the moon's weak gravity and slept. Except that she wasn't sleeping. Inessa turned the woman's head to see her ashen, grey face. Clouded eyes stared past her. Inessa touched the dead woman and her finger sank into the flesh, skin tearing like rice paper. She pulled her hand away out of pure reflex, before catching her breath and slowly rising.

They passed more bodies before reaching the control room. All the bodies lay as if at rest, all devoid of color. There were more in the control room, those still in the chairs in which they died. Jardin and Maria tried to access the computer system while Inessa searched the room. Alan provided light with two flashlights.

"It is no good," Jardin said. "Systems are absolutely dead." He looked at the man in the chair beside him, his lifeless eyes seeming to watch the Argentine. Jardin reached out to close the man's eyes, but his fingers tore his eyelids and sank into his eye balls. He pulled away.

"I am sorry, my friend," he said.

"I am getting absolutely no readings," Maria said from a nearby station "We need a power source to access data. Something fried theirs. And it may have fried anything on the computers."

"Let's hope not," Inessa said. "Locate the drive and bring it to the *Sunspot*. Hopefully the data is not corrupted."

The crew sat mutely around the messroom table. The days taken to decipher the damaged feed from Luna Base gave them more than enough time to assess the catastrophe. They sat transfixed by the grainy image on the viewscreen, watching the moment when humanity died. A light emerged from the sun, grew brighter as the seconds passed, and approached at terrific speed. A voice crackled in a message from Luna to earth, identifying the ship as the returning *Solar Flare*. Another crackle: a request to *Solar Flare* for communication. It was left unanswered. The ship flew closer to the planet, too quickly for any reaction except to watch in horror. A flash filled the screen as the *Solar Flare* tore into the planet's atmosphere, followed by a blinding explosion. Followed by static and nothing else. The feed rewound and they watched it again.

"That was the *Solar Flare*," Gunther said.

"It was accelerating," Dave added, as if to himself. "It continued to accelerate after the event. It would have been going ..." his voice trained away with his computation.

The crew watched the ship hit the earth, and the explosion that followed, again.

"Why would they continue to accelerate?" Dave asked nobody in particular, his thoughts tumbling out of his mouth unimpeded. "It's not possible. There are failsafes."

"That wasn't the *Solar Flare*," Maria said. "Not the crew. It couldn't have been."

"Even at that speed," Dave said, his voice already trailing off, "it could not have produced that explosion ..."

"The Nyrians," Inessa said.

"They waited three hundred years?" Gunther asked.

"They waited," Inessa repeated. "They waited because of us."

"That's not possible," Shu Len said. "They waited three hundred years?"

"Why would they do that?" Ariana whispered.

"Because of me," Inessa said. "Because I led us to the surface. Because I showed them who we were. All powerful aliens who can bend time and space."

"We all chose to land," Gunther said.

"I am the captain. I am responsible."

"They waited three hundred years?" Ariana asked again. "That's insane. That's not possible."

Inessa gestured at the ceiling, at what was outside the ship. "It is possible," she said.

"Are we sure that was the *Solar Flare*?" Abede asked.

"I examined the feed in detail," Eva said. "There is no doubt."

"But ... it's not possible," Ariana repeated.

"It is possible," Inessa said. "It is possible because of me—"

"Stop with the self-pity!" Alan interrupted. He pointed a finger at his captain. "Sitting here moaning and feeling sorry for yourself isn't going to help."

Inessa faced him, mouth open, and they grew quiet.

"Well?" Alan demanded.

"What are you doing, my friend?" Jardin asked.

"Nothing. Sitting here in the mess, crying and moaning, I am doing absolutely nothing! We are doing absolutely nothing!"

"Alan—" Shu Len tried.

"Fuck this," Alan said. "We don't have to just sit here feeling sorry for ourselves and wait to die."

"Alan—" Shu Len said again, placing a hand on his.

He pulled it away and held both his hands in the air. "We're all-powerful aliens who bend time and space!" he said. "We fix it."

"How do we fix it?" Thanh asked.

"Stop the Nyrians," Alan said.

"We couldn't stop the Nyrians, not if they could take the *Solar Flare*," Gunther said. "We are not military."

"Then we stop the *Solar Flare*. We can show up anytime we want. We can show up before the *Flare* decelerates and warn them." Alan noticed his hands, stopped gesticulating and lowered them to the table. "We can warn them before they even leave the solar system."

"How could do that? We leave earth at the same time," Ariana asked.

"That doesn't matter," Alan answered. "Time doesn't matter. We show up whenever we want to."

"We can stop ourselves," Inessa said softly.

"What do you mean?" Gunther asked.

"We stop ourselves from landing, from making contact," she replied. "We stop ourselves from going on the mission."

"We cannot do that," Jardin said.

"We can," Inessa insisted. "I know *I* would listen to myself if I came with a warning."

"Then what?" Jardin asked gently. "The two of you return to earth and divide your possessions? You know we cannot share time lines. It is not possible."

"We don't know that," Inessa replied. "It is only theory."

"It is not something you want to experiment with," Jardin said.

"Not even to save the earth, Jardin?"

"We stop the Nyrians," Eva said.

"We aren't military," Gunther insisted. "We don't know why or how, but even the crew of the *Solar Flare* could not—"

"Not those Nyrians!" Eva said, raising her voice. "We stop the message from ever being sent. No message, no contact, no ..." she pointed at the viewscreen, "no ... that. No message, no response, it never happened."

"We stop the message," Alan said, trying the idea on for size. He liked the fit.

"Making contact again?" Dave asked. "That's what got us here in the first place."

"They won't be waiting for us," Alan countered. "So, they won't detect us."

"Aliens walking among them? They won't detect that?"

"We stay away from the collective," Eva said. "We know where to go."

"The radio disc?" Ariana asked. "If the disc is built, it would be too late."

"No, before the disc. We stop the disc from ever happening," Alan said.

"Tauma would listen." Inessa spoke quietly, and to herself, but Alan heard and smiled at his captain.

"Tauma would listen to you," he agreed. "He would know you."

"We don't know that," Dave said. "We would be strangers to them. Aliens."

"No, we wouldn't," Alan said. "And you know that. We've known each other across time and space. That won't change. They were waiting for us before. They were always waiting."

"We could never go home," Maria said.

"We have no home," Gunther said. "It is out there, destroyed. Everything we knew, everybody we loved, is gone."

"No," Inessa said. "Not everyone we loved is not gone. We know where they are."

The table grew silent as the words sank in.

"Tauma will listen. He will know me, even if he hasn't met me yet," Inessa added.

"How will you find him?" Thanh asked. "How will we find any-body and not be detected?"

"Tauma will go to the cabin," Alan said. "We can land at a time when he will be there. And Inessa will find him. Then he will find the others and bring them to us. We can build a small settlement, right where it was. Away from everything. Away from everybody."

"What if they don't come?" Dave asked.

"They'll come," Alan said. "Salia will come, and she will know you. And this time we'll do it right, because we won't ever leave them."

23

Alan copied lines of poetry from his tablet as quickly as he could. He started with prompts, fragments of verse that would jog his memory later, when he had more time to lean and loaf at his ease. Now wasn't that time. He stopped scribbling as Maria sounded the thirty-minute alarm. Thirty minutes before the shuttle launched, leaving the surface of Nyria. No crew would accompany the craft as it docked in the larger ship, nor would any crew be on the *Flare* as she accelerated towards, and into, the sun. None would watch to see if it made its own flare as it destroyed itself. All technology beyond what was already developed on Nyria remained on the ship. Which included Alan's tablet, and the only copy of Whitman's *Leaves* digitally stored on it.

I believe a leaf of grass is no less than the journey work of the stars ... He left that line and moved on. It was enough to bring back more later. Ceera loved *Song of Myself*, after he explained that the opening lines were not about collective ownership of bodies, but celebrating hers with his individuality, willingly sharing, about joining, about connecting on a level transcending bodies.

"I celebrate myself," he said aloud in his quarters. He didn't write the line down because it was cemented in his mind. "And what I assume you shall assume, for every atom belonging to me as good belongs to you."

Dave passed his door with a small bag containing all his possessions, every item checked and approved by Jardin, acting captain while Inessa was away. Inessa took a small rucksack containing all her things, as well as all their hopes, and set out for the small hut in the mountains. Sometime tomorrow, or maybe even late tonight, a knock would sound on Tauma's door. She had a long walk to prepare what to say, to somehow tell him he needn't build a radio dish because he already did and she has answered his call.

"He will know me," she said as she left, more to herself than those seeing her off.

Alan scrolled through the long poem, stopping at a poem called *Faces*. She would enjoy that one, how it tours the people of the city, on a planet where all are individual and lost, where all sought union. He could spend hours explaining the imagery, and remember a home he would never see again. Maybe there was a Ceera somewhere reading it to herself, a Ceera in the not-so-distant future, hiding in the collective, hiding her difference and her secrets. Alan paused, remembering that the Ceera he hoped to meet would be a stranger. His mouth relaxed into a frown before he shook his head.

"No," he said aloud. *She will know me,* he said to himself.

He started writing again:

Sauntering the pavement or riding the country byroads here then are faces.

Faces of friendship, precision, caution, suavity, ideality,

The spiritual prescient face, the always welcome common benevolent face,

The face of singing music, the grand faces of natural lawyers and judges broad at the backtop,

The faces of hunters and fishers, bulged at the brows .... The shaved blanched faces of orthodox citizens,

The pure extravagant yearning questioning artist's face,

The welcome ugly face of some beautiful soul .... The handsome detested or despised face,

The sacred faces of infants

Alan's pen tore the paper as he started with fright at Jardin's voice.

"Ten minutes, my friend," Jardin said. "It is time."

"Just a few more minutes, I'll be ready."

"We don't have any more time."

"My bag is on the bunk," Alan said. "Check it. I'll grab a few more lines."

Jardin moved to the bunk and opened Alan's bag. There wasn't much there. He made sure any insignia were removed from the uniform, any advanced technology or modern comfort from home. He stuck a finger into Alan's sheepskin slippers, feeling for any contraband. He removed a small stone, examined it, and held it up.

"What is this?"

Alan stopped writing, reached up, grabbed it and put it in his pocket. "Just a stone," he said. "From here. It's special, something—"

"Alright," Jardin said. "It's okay. But now I need the tablet, and you need to leave the shuttle."

Alan looked at the half-copied poem, folded the paper and put it in his bag. He handed the device to Jardin and stood.

"I'll see you outside," Alan said.

He took the bag in one hand and stuck his other in his pocket, where it closed around the small stone. *I will give it to her when we meet,* he rehearsed in his mind again, *and she will understand. She will hold it against the one she already has and see they are the same, that it is a time travelling stone carried by her time travelling man. And ...*

He descended the ramp and joined his crewmates on a distant bank. After Jardin left, the hatch closed and the ramp retracted. He sat with them and watched as the shuttle stood upright, and then shot upwards. They followed the craft as it grew smaller and smaller, until it disappeared in the clouds far above.

Acknowledgements

Poetry extracts taken from *Leaves of Grass*, The First (1855) Edition by Walt Whitman, published by Penguin Books, 1959, reprinted in Penguin Classics, 1986.

The Nyrian creation story was inspired by the *Dialogues* of Plato, notably the human creation myth presented by Aristophanes in *The Symposium,* (circa 360 BCE).

ALSO BY CHRISTOPHER MCMASTER

Travel to the future with exciting science fiction and climate fiction from Southern Skies Publications (MisStep, Seeders, Journey to the Stars, and Pirates Come Down)

Travel to the past (and alternate realities) with the *Lucid* series from Dreaming Big Publications (American Dreamer, Tomorrow's History and Gods and Dreamers)

MISSTEP

S *tepping: The easiest way to get from point A to point B is to put A and B in the same place. Simply Step from one to the other. Known as an Einstein-Rosen bridge, it is theoretically possible. It just requires an immense amount of energy. And in a future where that energy is harnessed, that's what we do.*

Jens needed to get off the planet in a hurry so he took the first job on an interstellar freighter he found—part of a convoy to a far-flung mining colony, three Steps and almost three thousand lightyears away. Only the desperate went so far—colonists willing to trade a life on Earth for a new start on a rock somewhere across the galaxy, or spacers one step ahead of the law.

But as each Step takes him farther from home, Jens learns that the job isn't exactly what he was told, the cargo not as legitimate, and his situation even more precarious. Jens finds himself being groomed for a role in an interplanetary drug racket, with no way out.

Then the convoy mis-Steps, emerging lightyears off course, and the miscalculation might not be their fault!

seeders

The exciting sequel to MisStep:
They tried to hide from certain death. Now it's time to find them.

A pandemic spread over their planet and swept them from history. In a desperate act to save their species they launched a remnant of survivors into the depths of space, frozen in cryo-sleep, to be awakened only when their ship detected a habitable planet. But there were no planets and the ship continued into the cold and dark.

Thousands of years later humans have settled the ocean world. Earth's dream of finding her sister planet has come true, and it was free for the taking. They gave it their own name, *Pemako*, and lived beside the ruins of what was once a mighty civilization. Picking through the artifacts, xeno-linguist Peter Taylor and a small research team find evidence of the Original's desperate mission. Plotting the probable course of the ship, the team locate where it might be, if it really exists, and if it is still operational.

The promised technology of the Originals outweighs any 'ifs'. But they need the help of a powerful earth-based consortia, as well as from Andrew Jensen, the only man to ever survive a confrontation with those whose planet they now call their own.

Journey to the Stars

Science Fiction Stories from the Bottom of the Ocean to the Depths of Space

An alien ethnographer collects death moments for his study. One Autumn morning he starts to show Chloe ...

A man's dream of meeting the lights he has seen in the sky, of journeying with them, turns to nightmare when he finally gets what he wants ...

With an asteroid hurtling towards the planet, a ship is sent to evacuate a colony. There are some that don't want to leave ...

In the early days of NASA, they thought the vast emptiness and solitude would be too much for the human mind to handle. For this space trucker, maybe they were right ...

And more! Eighteen science fiction stories from the bottom of the ocean to the depths of space. With a unique look behind the scenes in a conversation with the author.

"A worrying glimpse inside my mind."—the author

Pirates Come Down

Science fiction meets climate fiction in this high seas thriller. Fishing in the future takes more than a net!

Rickets is a PAC man, his patrol and attack craft the first line of defence against encroaching vessels. Moss is a Fisheries Observer, tasked with ensuring that companies abide by the quotas set on target species. Together they play a part in seeing that the waters are not fished to extinction.

But as fisheries elsewhere play out, New Zealand waters start to look more attractive, until every ship protects itself with PAC boats, missiles that skim the surface, and kamikaze drones equipped with explosives.

Only there is a bigger shadow on the horizon, one that deflects all radar, is lethally armed, and takes what it wants!

American Dreamer

L ucid book #1: Can one person change a reality?
1944. President Roosevelt is ailing, and whomever is selected
as VP will end up leading the country. At stake is more than a candi-
date, more than a political office, but an entire timeline.

Waking in a dream Nadia finds herself in a classroom with two
other students. The woman posing as their teacher (if indeed she is
a woman), convinces them that they have no real choice but to assist
with her plan. Miss Biel breaks each of them with terrifying night-
mares, and 'tasks' to complete while awake that destroys any hope of
escape.

But Nadia begins to realize she isn't quite alone, not exactly pow-
erless, and that there are those besides Miss Biel who want a certain
outcome. There comes a time when she has to decide who to trust.

"A great story, imaginative and absorbing, I read the whole book
over a weekend, couldn't put it down. The crossing between alternate
universes and parallel lives was like American Gods written by Neil

Gaiman. It was a reminder that even in these troubled times, things could be worse!" —Amazon reviewer

TOMOrrOW'S HISTOry

L ucid book #2: Can one person save a reality?

London. Present day. The sun glints off solar panels, harvesting the energy that keeps the city moving. Roof gardens add a hint of green to the skyline. Airships pass overhead on their way north to the capital, Jorvik. Ships of the Great Fleet load at the busy docks, preparing for the voyage across the Western Ocean to the Far Settlements, holding the Norse world together.

Jakob would think his world is safe. But it isn't. Something needs finishing for his present to come to pass, and for some unknown reason he has been chosen to do it. Trapped in his dreams and thrust into an age of Vikings who are much more familiar with the sword and the axe, he lacks the one skill that is essential to survival. While the gods manipulate fate, he uses the only thing he has—his wits.

Tasked with leading a party of Danes in pursuit of royal game he is swept into an adventure that can only have one outcome if Britain is to survive. King Alfred "the Great" must not get away.

GODS anD DreamerS

Lucid book #3: Time kills all things, even the gods

We all dream. Only most of don't remember. How can we even know what we do in our dreams if the memory fades like mist when we wake up? Teeny, Robbie, and Thieu start to recall their dreams and the disturbing acts of violence and servitude that they are coerced into committing in timelines other than theirs.

Awareness breeds rebellion. Led by Petrit and Nadia, who enlist the new rebels into their secret campaign against the manipulative gods, the dreamers learn how to use their lucidity to resist the oppressive forces that control their dreams and realities alike. Together, the dreamers struggle to protect their timelines and push back against the gods that exploit mortals for entertainment and rewrite history for sustained nourishment.

But first they have to survive. There are others who think them heretics and will try to stop them at all costs.

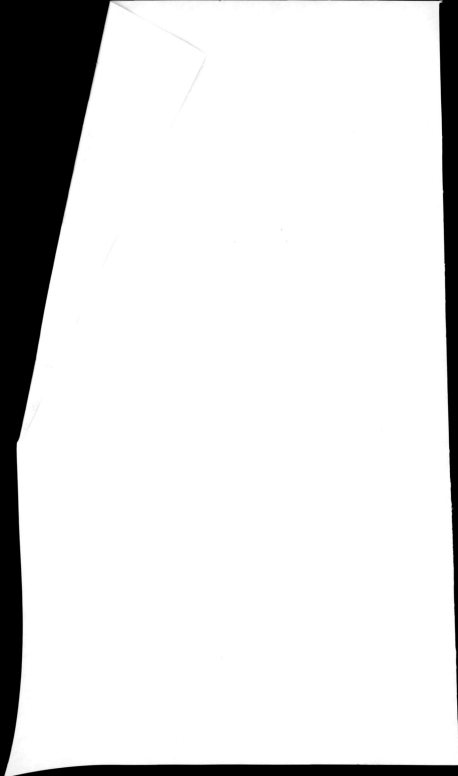

TO Learn more ABOUT CHRISTOPHER'S BOOKS, VISIT HIM AT:

www.christophermcmaster.com

Made in the USA
Middletown, DE
30 April 2023